I0451059

Feral

The Shelter Series, Book One

Kate Sherwood

About The Book You have Purchased

This story is a work of fiction. Names, characters, places, and incidents are either the product of the author's imagination or are used fictitiously to further the plot in this story. Any resemblance to actual persons living or dead, business establishments, events, or locales are entirely coincidental.

Cover Art by: A.J. Corza

website: www.ajcorza.com

Cover content is for illustrative purposes only and any persons depicted on the cover are models.

Formatting by: All Indie Publishing Services

website: www.allindiepublishingservices.com

Thank you for purchasing this book. Your purchase allows you ONE LEGAL printed copy for personal reading. ALL RIGHTS RESERVED. Duplication or distribution by any means is illegal and a violation of international copyright law. Violators of same are subject to criminal prosecution, and, upon conviction, fines and/or imprisonment. No part of this book may be reproduced or transmitted in any form or by any means, electronic or mechanical, including but not limited to: photocopying, recording, or by any information storage and retrieval system without the express written permission of the publisher and/or author, and where permitted by law. Reviewers and/or Bloggers may quote brief passages in a review or for promotional purposes, only. To request permission and all other inquiries, contact the author directly.

Feral

The Shelter Series, Book One

Copyright ©2015 Kate Sherwood

www.katesherwoodbooks.com

Feral

Noah Reed has his life planned out. There was that one glitch, years ago, but he's back on track now and determined to reach his goal of becoming a veterinarian and building his own practice.

Shane Black's hard life has taught him there's no point in looking forward and even less in looking back. He takes life as it comes, and his only real need is medical care for his young pup, Dodger.

When Shane stumbles into the clinic where Noah volunteers, Noah's instincts tell him to run away from the dangerous, unpredictable ruffian. But the puppy needs help, and maybe Shane does, too.

The young men soon discover that Dodger was poisoned, and so were several street people Shane knows. As they search for the source of the poison, Noah learns about the dark underside of the city where he's spent his whole life, and Shane learns that there is light in the world, even when he's stuck in the shadows.

But when their relationship begins to grow from a partnership to a romance, new challenges appear. Their worlds are so different—can they ever make sense together? Is there any room in Noah's carefully planned life for someone as unpredictable as Shane?

Word Count: 63,679
Genre: LGBTQ Contemporary Romance

Warning: This book contains graphic language and sexually explicit content. Intended for adult audiences only. Not intended for anyone under the age of 18.

Chapter One

THE CLINIC WAS ALL calming greens and blues, with plants and comfortable chairs in the waiting area. It was in a rough part of town and the ceiling sloped a bit in the far corner as if maybe the structure wasn't completely sound, but overall, the place looked nice, and that was no good at all.

"I'd need a payment plan or something," Shane Black said quickly. After the last two places he'd been, it only made sense to get that out of the way right from the start. If they weren't going to help him here, at least he could get on his way somewhere else without wasting much more time. Time was something he wasn't sure he had.

Luckily the middle-aged woman behind the counter, her blue uniform clearly matched to the décor, didn't seem alarmed by his statement. "That won't be a problem. Come this way, please."

It seemed too easy. After everything that had gone wrong, things were going right too fast. So Shane followed her, but he did it warily, waiting for things to go wrong again. Then everything would be back to normal and he'd be able to relax.

"You can put him on the table there," the woman said, and she waited while Shane reached inside his sweatshirt and pulled out the bundle of warm, dark fur. The pup had been so happy and energetic just a day before, but now he was almost limp in Shane's hand, barely able to raise his head. Shane swallowed hard. He'd been stupid to let himself get attached. He should have known better. He *had* known better, damn it. But he'd ignored his common sense, and now he was getting what he deserved. It just wasn't fair that the pup was being punished along with his owner.

He leaned down so his forearms made a wall around Dodger's little body. Not to keep the animal from escaping, but to—Shane didn't know. To keep him warm, to protect him. But again, that was being stupid, because whatever had gotten to this pup had already done its damage. And if Dodger was taking any comfort from Shane's presence, the pup was stupid, because he couldn't count on Shane to keep him safe. Obviously. Fuck!

"I need to weigh him," the woman said softly. "If you want, you can put him on the scale yourself." She gestured to a sort of platform on the stainless steel counter, and Shane eased his fingers back under Dodger's suddenly fragile body and lifted him as gently as he could. The pup's belly was tender and bruised-looking, and it was hard to find a way to touch him that didn't seem like it would hurt. Dodger raised his head again, found

Shane's face, and relaxed. He felt safe because Shane was there. What a stupid, stupid animal.

"You don't have a precise age for him?" the woman asked as she tapped away at a tablet screen.

"No. I've had him for a week and a half, about. I don't know how old he was when I found him, though."

"Not very." There was a note of disapproval in the woman's voice that Shane would have fought against at any other time, but right then he figured she was right. Dodger was too young to be away from his mother. Maybe Shane should have tried harder to get him back to his family, although he had no idea what he would have done. There had been three other puppies in the garbage bag Dodger had managed to claw his way out of, but they'd already been dead when Shane found them. No, whatever kind of asshole would do that to a litter of puppies wasn't someone Shane should have been returning an animal to. But he could have taken the little guy to a shelter, where he'd have been taken care of by people who knew what the fuck they were doing.

"What's he been eating?"

Shit, another question Shane was flushed with shame over. "Just— whatever. Bits of what I ate, usually. I got him a bag of puppy food—" Probably not a good idea to mention that Shane had smuggled it out of the grocery store under his hoodie— "but he liked my food better. I gave him milk sometimes."

"And his appetite was good until a couple days ago? No signs of intestinal distress?"

"No, he seemed fine."

There were a few more questions, and then the woman gave Shane a smile that was probably meant to be reassuring. "The doctor will be in shortly," she said. She headed for the door, then paused. "Puppies get sick sometimes. You can't protect them from everything, no matter how hard you try." Her voice was gentler than Shane deserved, but she was a bit more upbeat as she added, "And we just so happen to be *excellent* at making them better. So hang in there." She bent to the side as if trying to see past Shane and added, "You too, Dodger. We're going to help you out, okay?"

The puppy didn't even raise his head, but Shane managed to nod his own. He didn't deserve this woman's kindness and if he hadn't been so worried about Dodger he'd have had the strength to reject it. As it was, though? "Thank you," he whispered, and then he hunched over the dog again.

*****

Noah Reed tried to pay attention to the patient, not the owner. The puppy was clearly in serious distress and Dr. Anderson was giving him a thorough examination; Noah should have been following along and trying to make his own diagnosis. That was the whole point of him volunteering at the clinic.

But the owner was far too distracting. Tall, with rangy shoulders and big, strong hands that tightened into fists whenever he wasn't using them to cradle the puppy. Dark eyes in a face that looked tanned in spite of the grey weather, ripped jeans and a ragged hoodie, and a tattoo stretching from just below his left ear, around the back of his head and up beneath the shadow of his almost shaved hair. The inked image was something abstract and monstrous, wings and a gaping mouth and big, bulging eyes. And the guy wearing the tattoo was staring at Noah and Dr. Anderson as if he was about to pull a knife and start stabbing. Dr. Anderson was the expert and she could try to help the puppy; Noah had other priorities, like safety.

"So what's our next step?" Dr. Anderson asked him, and Noah tried to call himself back to the case.

"Uh... blood test?"

Dr. Anderson nodded, but with a squint that suggested she'd noticed Noah's lack of focus. She spoke to the thug, then. "We've definitely got internal bleeding. Based on the slower onset and the lack of visible injuries, we're probably looking at some sort of poison. We're going to do a blood test, take some x-rays, and then we'll start a transfusion to get some blood back in his veins where it belongs. Okay?"

"Poison?" the thug asked. His voice was a low growl, an accusation. "What kind of poison?"

"The tests will help confirm that," the vet said, pulling out the tools for taking blood as she spoke. "But the most likely culprit is some sort of rodenticide. Mouse or rat poison."

"And if that's what it is?" The thug kept his chin high, his body braced as if he was anticipating a physical blow, and Noah felt the first glimmer of sympathy for him.

"If that's what it is, we have a clear and very successful treatment plan. Working with puppies is always a bit more delicate, but if I'm right about what we're looking at, the poison robs the body of vitamin K, which is essential to blood clotting. So we can just help Dodger with some vitamin supplements until the poison is out of his system."

"That easy?" The thug sounded suspicious.

But Dr. Anderson nodded calmly. "Honestly, at this stage, I'm hoping for that diagnosis, because it *is* the easiest to treat. There are a few other possibilities, but this is the place to start."

So Noah helped draw the blood, and set up the transfusion. He was just a volunteer and Dr. Anderson didn't let him do much besides cleaning without close supervision, but she was really good about letting him try new things when she was around. The puppy, a black and brown furball that was probably some sort of terrier cross, was too weak to object to the procedures. Sad, but his lethargy actually made the treatment a bit easier, and Noah was pleased with his ability to find a good vein.

He stepped back from the table after taping down the needle that would carry the transfusion and smiled in satisfaction. But the happiness faded when he saw the thug glaring at him. "You enjoying yourself?" the guy demanded. "Sticking needles into puppies is your idea of a good time?"

"What? No! I mean—what are you talking about? I'm just glad it worked!"

"What wouldn't have worked?" the thug demanded.

Dr. Anderson stepped in smoothly. "The procedure was a little delicate because Dodger is small and dehydrated. That makes it harder to find a vein, but it went well. You can stay with him, if you like, and we'll go run some tests and see where we're at."

The thug was glowering at both of them, now, and Noah found himself worrying about violence again. Someone like that? The guy obviously wasn't too preoccupied with following society's rules, and that could totally include the rule about not stabbing people who were helping you.

But Noah and Dr. Anderson made it out of the room safely. They didn't speak until they were down the hall in the small on-site lab, where Noah said, "Okay, that owner's a bit scary. You think it's a good idea, leaving him alone in the exam room? I mean, there's not a *lot* to steal, but—"

"Noah." Just two syllables, but there was enough weight to it to silence him. She shook her head. "You know what this clinic is about, and you know my expectations. We help everyone. It's our job to look after the animals, but we need to have good relationships with the humans, too. And a good relationship means being respectful."

Noah wasn't going to argue with her, and possibly he'd been a bit over the top, worrying that the guy was going to steal anything. But the way people presented themselves was a message to others, and the message this guy was sending, with his clothes and his tattoos and his glare? It was a clear warning.

"So, have you done a clotting profile before?" Dr. Anderson asked.

Right. That was why Noah was at the clinic, to get hands-on experience and learn things. Not to worry about hot, angry thugs.

Wait, hot? Where the hell had *that* come from?

"Noah? Clotting profile?"

"Uh, no. Haven't done one," he managed. Clotting profile. Puppy blood, for goodness sake! *That* was what he needed to be thinking about. Puppy blood wasn't sexy, it wasn't dangerous, and at least in this limited context, it wasn't forbidden. "Can you walk me through it?"

Dr. Anderson agreed, and Noah got to work. Puppy blood was all he needed to think about.

Chapter Two

BY THE TIME THE clinic was closing down for the night and Shane had to leave Dodger behind, the puppy had found enough strength to whine piteously as he was shut away in a cage. The sound was bittersweet: good that the dog was able to create that much noise, but horrible to think that after all his physical suffering he was now going to be suffering emotionally, too.

"He's exhausted and he'll be asleep five minutes after we leave," the woman from behind the counter said firmly. She'd introduced herself as Martha sometime in the mid-afternoon, but Shane wasn't sure if he wanted to think of her that way. Learning her name meant thinking of her as a person, and his life was a lot easier if he tried to ignore as much of the humanity that surrounded him as possible.

"Someone's going to check on him, though? He won't be here alone all night?" Dodger was used to sleeping snuggled inside Shane's sweatshirt, and the thin towel in his cage just wasn't a good substitute for a warm body.

"It's six o'clock now, and a tech comes by just after midnight to give meds and check on everybody. Then we're open again at eight."

Seven hours between the visits. If something went wrong, Dodger would be alone. No one to help him, no one to comfort him. Dying would be bad enough, but dying by himself? Dogs were pack animals. They needed their buddies with them, especially when times were rough.

So Shane allowed himself to be herded out the front door of the clinic, and he tried to look casual and relaxed as he headed down the street. It wasn't his usual part of town, but he was used to paying attention to his surroundings. He knew where he was going. But first he had to kill some time.

He found a dingy grocery store half-way down the block, one of the kind with fruits and vegetables displayed along the sidewalk like the people running the store were living in the nineteen fifties or were back in whatever Old Country they'd come from. There were some yellowish oranges on sale and he took two of those, then went inside to pick up a few packages of instant ramen noodles. A tired-looking woman had started tracking him as soon as he came into the store and she looked mean enough he was tempted to just take the food and run; he didn't like stealing from nice people, but he didn't mind doing it from someone like her. But he still had some cash in his pocket, and he didn't usually steal until he was dead broke.

A man needed some sort of principles, he figured. So he counted out his coins and scowled at the woman as he left.

He was protected from scurvy and had some good, cheap carbs, all for a couple bucks. The noodles might be a bit tastier if he had a stove to cook them on, but they were okay raw, too.

He stuffed his dinner inside his sweatshirt and headed back the way he'd come. Turned the corner, cruised into the alley like he had a legit reason to be there, then counted the different buildings and doorways until he was back where he wanted to be. The door was metal, and pretty solid, but the lock was cheap. The staff had all been packing up and pulling their coats on as he'd left, and while he'd noticed motion detectors that suggested a security system in the front rooms, there'd been nothing in the back. There'd be too many animals shifting around in their cages at night to make motion detectors practical.

At least, that was what he hoped.

He probably could have managed the lock with a straightened out paper clip, but he pulled out his set of picks anyway. They'd been a gift from Uncle Davey before the poor bastard got sent away, and it was a good tribute to use them from time to time. Of course, Davey wouldn't be too impressed with Shane using them to break into a vet clinic and hang out with a damn puppy, but Davey wasn't around to be judgemental about that sort of thing.

So Shane got to work, taking deep breaths to keep his body relaxed and his hands steady as he felt for the tumblers.

Maybe there was a part of his brain telling him how stupid this was, but he'd gotten really, really good at ignoring that voice. Another thought, not quite as easy to move past, reminded him that the vet and the other woman—Dr. Anderson and Martha, and, damn it, he wished he didn't know their names—had been kind to him, and to Dodger. *Easy to be nice when you have all the power and all the money*, he told himself. *And you're not hurting them just by hanging out with Dodger. You're not breaking anything, and he's your dog. Your responsibility.*

Still, even after he got the door unlocked, he didn't open it right away. Being careful about alarms, of course. Checking to be sure no one had wandered into the alley to see him go inside. Just being cautious, not dealing with his conscience. Not him.

He was still on the low concrete ramp, the door only open a couple inches, when he heard a gentle noise from inside. A whimper, a whine—Dodger, sensing him, and wondering why the hell he wasn't coming closer.

"Hey, buddy," Shane whispered, and he slipped through the doorway, making sure it shut tightly behind him. "You okay?"

He heard the puppy stir and moved fast, over to the cage to stick his fingers through the metal bars. It wouldn't be good if the little guy ripped out his IV or something. A wet tongue found Shane's fingers, sharp puppy teeth nipped a greeting, and the tight ball in Shane's stomach eased at least somewhat. Dodger was happy to see him, and feeling healthy enough to let him know. Everything was okay.

The puppy lay back down without the wriggling and begging for freedom that would have shown he was truly well again, but he just seemed tired, not sick.

Someone was coming in just after midnight, Shane reminded himself. Probably best to be sure he was gone by eleven thirty, and then he could watch the building and see when the tech arrived and left. He could sneak back in then, get a few hours of sleep after checking on the pup, and be out again before the staff arrived in the morning.

"Everything's okay, buddy," he told Dodger, and the puppy didn't argue.

*****

"I got to do the IV for the transfusion, too." Noah leaned back, making the ancient wooden chair creak in complaint, and laced his hands triumphantly behind his head. "It's harder with little puppies, you know, especially when they're as dehydrated as this one was. But I found a vein first try."

"Mom, tell him to stop talking about veins at the dinner table," Sarah groaned. She was fifteen, and her family communication tended to alternate between whining like a toddler and insisting she be treated as an adult. "He thinks he's cool because he stuck a needle into a defenseless little puppy! It's sick."

"I *saved* that defenseless little puppy," he said. Sarah wasn't going to bring him down. "He was sick, but I made him better. I'm a damn healer."

Sarah rolled her eyes, but their mother smiled at him. "I think it's wonderful. You're learning so much working with Dr. Anderson."

"Volunteering," Sarah clarified. "It's not like they actually pay him or anything."

"It's still work." Mrs. Reed's expression was warm and proud and shouldn't have made Noah sad. His mother never wanted him to be sad, and he always hoped she'd get what she wanted, so he needed to smarten up. He wasn't letting her down, not anymore. He was the son she wanted, the son she deserved, and he damn well always would be.

"Whatever," Sarah said, clearly ready to move on. "I need the form signed for the trip to the zoo by Monday or I can't go. And I need the payment, too."

"I don't really understand why you're going to the zoo." Mrs. Reed laid her fork down, abandoning the last couple mouthfuls of potato on her plate. "What's the point of the trip? What are you supposed to be learning?"

"Noah went when he took this class! Did Saint Noah have to explain what he was going to be learning?"

"Noah has wanted to be a veterinarian since he was old enough to say the word. Taking a trip to look at animals made sense, for him. If he'd wanted to go to—to a fashion warehouse or something, I'd have asked him why he thought it was an important trip."

14

"Yeah, sure you would have."

"Watch your tone, Sarah," his mother said firmly. "I don't care for sarcasm, and if you can't speak respectfully, you can leave the table."

"Great," Sarah said. Her eyes were filling with tears. "I can go call Alisha and tell her my mom won't let me go on the stupid trip!"

"Oh, cut the drama." Mrs. Reed sounded tired, but not exhausted enough to just lie down and tolerate nonsense. Noah didn't think she'd ever been that tired in her whole life. "If you want to discuss this politely, come back and we'll talk. But if you just want to flounce—I guess you're right, and you'd better call Alisha."

And then, as he'd known she would, Sarah whirled toward Noah. "This is all your fault! If you hadn't screwed up—"

"You being a drama queen isn't my fault," he told her as dryly as he could manage. "And that's all that's going wrong right now. Mom hasn't said you can't go on the trip, she just wants to—"

"I don't need an interpreter, thanks." Sarah pushed away from the table so hard her chair almost fell over. "I don't need any of this!" And she turned and stomped away from the table. Noah and his mother sat quietly until the slam of her bedroom door rattled through the small house.

"Have you ever noticed that she has most of her tantrums on the nights it's her turn to do the dishes?" Noah asked, standing up and starting to stack plates.

"It's not easy being fifteen," his mother said. Then she grinned in a way that let him know what she must have looked like when she was fifteen herself. "But, yes, I *have* noticed the connection to the dishes. You can leave them for her, if you want."

He shook his head. It wasn't worth the fuss when she came out and found her chore still there, waiting.

Besides, if he was honest with himself, at least some of the current issue *was* because of him. Because he'd screwed up. His mom did the books for half the businesses in the neighborhood, and she'd made enough money for their small family to live fairly comfortably for most of his life. But not enough money to pay for the medical bills and the lawyers on top of his tuition. Not enough to pay for all that *and* unnecessary field trips to the damn zoo.

"I'm working breakfast and dinner Saturday, and dinner Sunday, and I get paid on Monday." He gathered the dishes off the table and kept his gaze averted from hers. "I can pay for the zoo."

"You need to be saving for next semester's tuition," she said firmly, pushing herself to her feet. "If there's an actual reason for the zoo trip and if she can discuss it like a civilized human being, I'll pay for it. If there isn't or she can't? Whatever. She's the one who blew through her babysitting money so fast."

It wasn't a big deal, he told himself as he turned the water on and filled the sink. There were people living in war zones, people without enough to eat right there in Seattle. A girl not going on a field trip was the furthest thing from a tragedy. And the last time he'd tried to apologize for his past mistake, his mom had gotten so mad she'd cried. She'd said she was sick of hearing about it, sick of thinking about it, and sick of seeing him creeping around like he was apologizing for his own existence. When she got mad, she tended to make pretty dramatic speeches. His high school English teacher would have been impressed with her use of parallelism or repetition or whatever the hell it was, but Noah? He'd just wanted her to stop crying.

And he didn't want her to start again now, so he kept his head down and focused on the dishes. When he was done cleaning up, he'd go study, because that was how someone like him spent his Friday nights. And he'd work his tail off at the restaurant the next day, trying to be the kind of flirty, outgoing person who earned big tips, and he'd keep everything on track. And as hard as it was, he'd stop apologizing. At least externally. At least for a while.

*****

Shane didn't like sleeping outside. Partly it was the weather: November in Seattle was wet and cold, and his layers of clothing didn't help much once they got soaked through. But he could handle that. What he really didn't like was being exposed. As soon as he closed his eyes, he was vulnerable. He'd learned that lesson when he was thirteen, the first time he'd been on his own on the streets. He'd walked until he was exhausted, then crawled in between a dumpster and a brick wall and laid down. He'd woken to find a stranger straddling him, rough, strong hands burrowing beneath his clothing to his bare skin.

It had just been a clumsy thief, that time, someone looking for the meagre cash hidden in Shane's front pocket. But there were other people on the streets at night, looking to steal more than money. So even though he'd turned into a very light sleeper, Shane still didn't want to close his eyes anywhere they could get him.

There were a couple places he could go, friends with rooms or even apartments where he could stay for a night or two, especially if he brought some weed or a bottle of something with him, but none close to the vet. Tristan was always welcoming, but he was also always kind of nosy and unfailingly practical. If he knew what Shane was doing he'd try to talk him out of it, and Shane didn't need that complication. So he huddled in a doorway across the street from the clinic front door and watched an unfamiliar woman let herself in around one and leave about an hour later. Then he circled back around through the alley, re-picked the lock, and found Dodger again. "You're doing great, buddy," he said, and after a few more greetings, Dodger went back to sleep and Shane slumped to the floor beneath the cage, propped his arms on his bent knees and his head on his arms, and let his eyes close.

He woke to the sounds of movement in the front of the clinic. Damn it!

He reacted fast, over to the door, quickly out into the alley, and then froze before he let the door close all the way. There was no way he'd been asleep for all that long. He looked down at the battered watch he'd been wearing since he was a kid. Four fifteen. It was quarter past four in the morning, and someone was in the front of the clinic.

It was none of his goddamn business, of course.

It could be someone who was supposed to be there; Martha had given him the we-check-on-your-pet speech, but she hadn't told him the entire security program for the building.

And even if it *was* someone who shouldn't be there, they weren't going to mess with a random puppy. Life wasn't a Disney movie, and Dodger wasn't a Dalmatian.

Yeah, whatever was going on in the front of the clinic was a great big case of Not Shane's Business. Still, he didn't let the door close all the way.

Breaking into a vet clinic to steal drugs was hardly unheard of. And this clinic wasn't in a great part of town, and Shane's own activities made it clear the security wasn't too intense. The place was an easy target.

Special K had started as a horse tranquilizer, he'd heard. This clinic probably didn't treat horses, but maybe they had ketamine in stock anyway. That'd be pretty valuable, to the right people.

But, shit. Hadn't the vet said she was treating Dodger with Vitamin K? What if the junkie assholes in the front room were too stupid to know that *Special* K and Vitamin K weren't the same thing?

He looked at the thin line of shadow where the door stood ajar from the wall. He could still go back in, without messing around with the picks.

There was no reason for it, really. He didn't really know anyone had broken in, he didn't know they were after ketamine, and it was a hell of a stretch to think they'd steal Dodger's medicine just because it had a letter in common with the street name of a popular drug. Even if they did steal it, the vet could probably just buy some more. All the same, Shane eased the door back open.

The room was still dark, but Dodger whined a little, looking for some attention. If Shane wasn't careful the dog was going to turn into a total suck, but he wasn't going to worry about that while the little guy was sick. And, shit, he wasn't going to worry about it while he was twenty feet away from random strangers who might be in the middle of committing a crime.

He eased closer to the door that led to the front of the clinic. The door had a window, and he peaked through to see the lights still off. But then the circle of a flashlight danced across the floor before jerking back to play on something out of sight.

A flashlight? Fuck that. No reason for a legit visitor to be using a damn flashlight.

Shane took a deep breath. *Stupid, stupid, stupid,* his inner uncle told him, apparently beaming his thoughts all the way from prison.

Shut up, Shane beamed back, *Or at least tell me something I don't already know*. Then he took another deep breath and threw the door open. "Hey!" he yelled, trying to channel the voice of authority that had been used against him far too many times. "What are you doing in here?"

Moment of truth, then. He braced himself for the gunshot, thought too late of what the hell Dodger would do without Shane to take care of him, then saw that there were two shapes behind the beam of the flashlight.

So he was outnumbered, but at least bullets weren't flying. Yet.

The shapes were moving fast, though, and he realized that he was between them and the front door. *Jesus Christ*, inner uncle yelled at him. *Have you ever thought a single thing through in your goddamn life?*

Well, he was smart enough to step back a little, giving the intruders room to pass by him. And the first one did, but the second guy was a bit bigger, a bit slower, and he was holding the flashlight. It beamed into Shane's face for a brilliant, disorienting moment, and then swung away. Oh, shit. The beam of light had changed direction, but the flashlight itself, the heavy metal weight of it? Shane couldn't see it so much as sense it, swinging down at him, everything in slow motion so even as he tried to dodge he knew he was too late. And then an explosion as the flashlight cracked him across the face somewhere between his cheekbone and his temple, too damn close to his eye.

He responded to pain just like he always did. His first swing caught the asshole somewhere in the ribs, and as the guy doubled over Shane grabbed the back of his head and jerked it down, right into Shane's rising knee. Then it was just the natural progression. Shane swung back with an elbow to his enemy's ear, let him stumble to his knees, kicked him in the ass, the thigh, whatever was handy as the man scrabbled and scrambled forward, away from pain, toward the door.

The savage joy of victory made Shane's chest feel like it might explode. This. This he could control. This fight wasn't stacked against him before he was even born, this battle was simple and clear and fair. And Shane had won, and he wanted to keep winning. He wanted to chase after the pathetic worm who'd challenged him, who'd caused him pain, maybe even made him bleed. A fight wasn't settled by retreat; it was settled by absolute victory, the sort that left one man lying in the dirt.

He managed to come back to himself even before he heard the siren. He'd won. The intruders were gone, the front door swinging shut behind them, and that was all he needed. He'd done what he was meant to do.

And, shit, the cops were coming. The back of the clinic wasn't alarmed, but the front almost certainly was. The idiots had set something off when they broke in.

Shane ducked back into the room with the cages, then took a moment to slip his fingers in toward Dodger. "You're okay, buddy. Everything's cool." A warm tongue reassured Shane that his message had been received, and then he moved, practically running until he hit the door, switching to cool and casual as he slipped outside and shut it tight behind him. A quick walk down the alley, ready to turn it into a sleepy shuffle as soon as anyone was paying attention to him.

You're an idiot, his uncle told him, but the adrenaline made it easy to ignore the old bastard. Shane had fought. He'd won. And he'd escaped. Everything else? He'd deal with it later.

Feral

Chapter Three

"WE NEED THIS CLEANED up," the woman said to Noah, her tone making it crystal clear exactly who she thought should be doing the cleaning. "You can't expect my child to just keep on eating with that sitting in front of him."

"No, ma'am," Noah said quickly. It wasn't like the restaurant *wanted* to leave kid-puke sitting in the dining room. "The busboy is coming to give you a clean tray."

"We need more than a clean tray. His meal is ruined."

Which was true, given that the kid had puked all over his grilled cheese breakfast. "Okay. I can get the kitchen to make another sandwich for him."

Noah's ingratiating smile bounced right off the woman's granite frown. He tried to remind himself of how difficult it must be to parent a toddler, and when that didn't do anything to improve his attitude, he worked on his other, more traditional mantra: *Tips. Tips. Tips.*

"I'm really sorry about this," he said as he headed for the

kitchen. It was true enough. He was sorry she'd brought her pukey child out in public, sorry she'd chosen to sit in his area of the restaurant, sorry he was too broke to be able to tell her to clean up her own kid's mess and leave the rest of them the hell alone. Yeah, he was sorry, all right.

"I need a kid's number seven," he told the cook. "Comp. The first one got messed up." Sergei was a good enough guy, a recent arrival from some Slavic state. He was quick to get things done when he wanted, slow as hell when he didn't, and his raised eyebrow was about as much of an objection as he ever offered. He showed it now, giving Noah a long, questioning look to go along with it.

"The kid threw up on it. I know, it's not our kid so it shouldn't be our problem, but if you want to deal with the mom, you can go right ahead."

The cook's quick grin showed that he'd decided to understand English, at least for the moment. "You're afraid of women, now?"

"Hell, yeah, I am. You can go fight with her if you want."

"For a grilled cheese?" Sergei's accent made the order sound like something exotic and daring, not that Noah should be noticing that sort of thing. "No. I will make a new number seven."

"Thank you."

"But the mother will not be happy," the cook warned, his smile far too winsome for the situation. "She does not want cheese on bread. What she does want, you can't give her."

Noah shook his head. "She just wants a damn grilled cheese meal and she doesn't want to pay for it. You're going to make that, right? So, yeah, I can give her that."

Sergei looked almost pitying, but at least he nodded. "I will grill the cheese. Comp. But it will not make her happy."

Noah was inclined to agree, but he let it go. He'd give up on the tip from that table, and just try to avoid getting the woman mad enough to complain to management. He wouldn't get his tip, but he'd keep his job. It was scant consolation, but it was what he could realistically hope for. "Thanks," he told the cook, who merely raised an eyebrow.

This was Sergei's life, Noah realized as he exchanged a sympathetic look with the puke-carrying busboy and then headed back out on the floor with an order for one of his other tables. For Noah, the service industry was a stepping stone, a way to earn some cash for tuition and maybe even extras, if his guilt didn't make him hand any surplus cash to his mother.

For Sergei? The man was already in his thirties, he was still working on his English, and he had no observable skills outside the kitchen. He was going to be a damn cook for the rest of his life, putting up with bullshit from people who wanted to blame others for their puking children. For Noah, this life was temporary. For Sergei? This was it.

"The new meal is on its way," Noah told the angry mother as he paused at her table. "I'm really sorry for the inconvenience."

She glowered at him, and he tried to contain it all as he went to his next table and forced another smile onto his face. "What can I get for you all today?" he asked. This was his job. It was his present, but not his future. It was what he did, not who he was.

All sorts of rationalizations. So many ways to justify being treated like a lesser life form. He just needed to keep his eyes on the prize. Some day, he'd rise above all this. He'd have his own life, his own career. He was just going through a painful period of transition.

"Water for everyone?" he echoed politely. They were too cheap too even buy coffee? That meant they wouldn't be tipping, either. "Okay, great. I'll be right back with that, and I can take your orders then."

Everything was fine, he told himself as he headed for the serving station. Everything was on track. He'd had his moment of madness, his one explosion, and it had hurt his family, hurt him, and achieved absolutely nothing. One deviation could be excused. But he wouldn't allow himself to fail again.

*****

"I'm just saying, I could use a bit more work, if you've got it." Shane kept his voice relaxed and easy. He wasn't begging—he'd steal before he begged—he was asking for a favor. It was a subtle but important difference.

And Moby's nod was respectful enough to make Shane feel the difference had been noticed. "You've done good work for me. You're a good kid. But it's better for the juvies to run the shit around, you know?"

Shane did know. He'd been one of the juvies himself, making deliveries of whatever Moby told him, wherever it was wanted, and bringing the cash back with him. He'd known that if he got caught he wouldn't face a serious consequence because of his age, and Moby had therefore known that Shane wouldn't be tempted to rat him out in exchange for a lesser charge. Once pot got legalized, business dried up some, but there were still pills and harder drugs to deliver. Then Shane had turned eighteen, and things had changed.

"I can do more of the other stuff, then. The parties, or even the streets if you want."

"I've got people working all the parties I can find, boy. And the streets? Since the fuckers pushed the legalization shit, you can't make a living as a street dealer." Moby looked away for only a moment, but it was long enough for Shane to know what was going to come next. "You want to do the other kind of work, I can still set you up with some of that. I know a couple guys who aren't into the skinny little fags I've got, but they'd be all over you. Maybe a bit rough, but there's more money that way, right?"

Shane nodded. More money if they got rough. And he needed money. He'd done it before, and if he had to, he'd do it again. "Not yet," he said. "I've got a few other things I should try first." And if he did decide to turn tricks, he'd do it without Moby taking a cut. The dealer might know a few guys who'd be interested, but Tristan could hook him up, too, and he'd do it as a favor, not for a percentage.

"Well, fuck off, then," Moby said without heat. "You woke me up pretty fucking early just to tell me you don't want work."

"I'll deal for you," Shane said. "If you've got *that* kind of work, I'm in."

"I'll keep you in mind," Moby said, and then he looked pointedly at the door to his apartment. Time for Shane to leave.

So he did. There were a couple other people he wanted to track down in his quest for money, but he let his feet carry him toward the clinic instead. It would be smart to stay away from the place after the mess the night before, but as long as they had Dodger, he'd have to show his face eventually, so he might as well get it over with.

And everything seemed pretty calm when he pulled the front door open and looked inside. Martha was there behind the counter, just as she'd been the day before, talking to an older couple who were holding the leash of a tiny dog. The little dog saw Shane and growled fiercely, his hackles bunching as he took a stiff-legged step forward.

"Okay, tough guy," Shane said softly, and stepped back. The dog probably weighed five pounds and wouldn't likely have the strength to bite through Shane's jeans, let alone his skin, but it wasn't Shane's place to make the little guy *feel* small. So he waited at a safe distance, and when the owners finished their business and left, the nipper trotted out beside them, proud of his guard dog status.

Martha turned her attention to Shane and said, "Dr. Anderson wants to see you. She's with a patient now, but—" She stopped, then quickly said, "Dodger's fine, Shane! He's doing well. That's not what she wants to talk to you about."

He tried to take a deep breath into a chest that had seized up a moment earlier and still wasn't ready to relax. Dodger was fine. And there were no cops, so this wasn't anything to do with the night before. The vet probably wanted to talk about a payment plan, which wasn't going to be a fun conversation, but was better than the alternatives. He managed a nice deep breath, then said, "Can I wait with Dodger, or should I stay out here?"

"I'm sure Dodger would be happy to see you," Martha said. She nodded toward the back rooms. "You know the way."

He was being paranoid to think there was anything extra in the way she said those words. He knew the way because he'd been in the building for hours the day before, that was all. She didn't know he'd come back.

Or maybe she did, and the cops were on the way.

He thought about grabbing Dodger and taking off. The pup was better, after all. But, no, the vet had said he'd need medicine for at least a month, and more testing, too.

He could be a fugitive himself, but not with Dodger.

And he wasn't going to abandon the pup. So he'd just have to deal with whatever the vet came up with.

The door to the room with the cages was open, and he stopped in the doorway. The assistant guy from the day before, the preppy kid who'd been so cheerful about sticking needles into Dodger's skinny little leg, was in there, spraying down a cage two doors away from Dodger. The guy hadn't noticed Shane yet, and he was talking to himself—no, wait. He was talking to Dodger.

"You're going to be out of here soon," he was saying. He was scrubbing the empty cage with one hand, but the other was stretched out, the fingers tickling Dodger's chin through the bars. "We'll get rid of all those tubes, and you'll just take some pills and you'll be fine. But you need to watch what you eat from now—" He broke off when he pulled his head out of the empty cage and saw Shane in the doorway. "Oh." He pulled his fingers away from Dodger almost guiltily. "I was just talking to him. Just nonsense, obviously—I know he can't understand the words."

"I talk to him all the time," Shane said. Dodger had noticed him now and was standing up, shoving his nose through the bars of the cage. Three long steps and Shane was there, letting Dodger chew on his fingers, trying not to let the immense relief he was feeling overwhelm him and make him do something humiliating. "He really is better," he managed, and the stranger probably didn't know that Shane's voice wasn't usually quite that gruff.

"Kind of amazing, isn't it? I mean, the transfusion was pretty important, but other than that, it's just vitamins."

"He's doing very well," a female voice said from behind them, and Shane turned to see Dr. Anderson in the doorway he'd just left. "He's strong. You must have been taking good care of him before he got sick."

"Not good enough, or he wouldn't have found the poison." And that was the unavoidable truth of the situation.

But the vet shook her head. "Puppies find things. They explore their world with their mouths, just like human babies, but a puppy's world is much less controlled. The only way to be absolutely sure he wouldn't come into contact with something like this would be to never take him outside, or muzzle him while he was going for walks or something. There are things we can do to minimize the risk, but we can't avoid it entirely." Her smile was kind, but changed to something more businesslike when she added, "Speaking of minimizing risk—can you come sit with me for a few minutes? There's something we need to discuss."

Yeah, they needed to minimize the risk of him running off without paying her. *He* might know he was determined to get her the money, one way or another, but she had no reason to trust him. So he pulled his fingers away from Dodger and followed the vet down the hall, feeling like he was being sent to the principal's office for an infraction he'd absolutely committed and couldn't begin to excuse.

She stopped outside a door at the far end of the hallway, unlocked it with a key from her pocket, then flipped the light switch inside the door before stepping inside. He followed her cautiously.

It was some sort of storage room. No windows, maybe eight by eight feet, and full of cardboard boxes. It seemed like a strange place to discuss debt repayment.

"Close the door," she said calmly.

There was something weird going on, he was pretty sure, but it wasn't like she was a physical threat. So he closed the door and stood there, waiting.

"We had some trouble here last night," she said.

Shit. But, okay, he knew the drill. Deny, deny, deny. "Did you?" he asked neutrally. He could feel the adrenaline starting to pump through his body. Fight or flight, and he wasn't so far gone that he'd beat up the woman who'd saved his dog, so that meant he needed to get the hell out of there. He needed to run. But he made himself stand still. Maybe he could still bluff it out.

The vet nodded, still relaxed. "A couple guys broke in. Junkies, probably, because they headed straight for our drug cabinet."

"Oh."

"Yeah. But then something really interesting happened, and they took off."

"Something interesting?" He was pretty sure his calm act was starting to crack at the edges, but he tried to stick with it.

"Interesting," she confirmed. "I can show you the video if you want, but I probably don't have to, right?"

"Video?" He sent the order to his muscles to relax, but they ignored him.

"Yeah, we have security cameras. Not many of them, and they don't pick up too much when the lights are off. But we got enough to see more or less what happened. I showed the video to the cops."

He was out of words. There were no windows in the room. Were there cops just outside the door, waiting for him? He could grab her, use her as a shield so he could fight his way free. *But she'd helped Dodger.* Shit.

She was watching him closely, and he felt like she could read his thoughts. "I told them we'd been worried about this sort of thing, so we'd hired a night watchman. I told them the watchman was the one who interrupted the theft." She gave him a look that was a lot more intense than he felt ready to deal with, then softened a little. "I told them it was our watchman who took a crack from the guy's flashlight, right across the side of his face." She reached out, then. He forced himself not to shy away, and her fingers were cool and light as they ghosted over the bruise Shane could feel but not see on himself. "Right there."

He felt almost dizzy. What the hell was she saying? Where was this going?

She pulled her hand back and smiled at him, cheerfully businesslike again. "They said it was a really good idea to have someone here overnight. And I agree with them. So, Shane, what I'm suggesting is that you work off Dodger's bills by spending your nights here. You can clear out these boxes—they're mostly just old records and paperwork from who knows when, and they've been sitting in here because nobody wanted to bother throwing them out. So you can load them in my car and I'll drop them off at the shredding station on my way home. Then we could get a bed, and there's already a shower in the staff bathroom—once spring comes and people start biking to work more often it'll get more use—and there's a fridge and a microwave in the office that you could use. You'd mostly be sleeping, but we'd give you some chores to do, probably—checking on the animals in between tech visits, obviously, and just keeping an eye on the place in general. But since you'd be sleeping most of the time, we probably wouldn't pay you all that much. You and I could negotiate something fair, I think. And then if you're interested, I have another job, more of a job-job that you might want to consider. But that's more my wife's project, so I'd like to wait for you to hear about it from her, if that's okay."

It was a trick, obviously. There was something—something illegal about it? Not that he really cared, but he at least wanted to know what it was. Or was it simpler than that? Was she just trying to get him talking, get him trusting her, so he'd confess about the night before? His mind raced, but he really wasn't good at thinking things through.

Best to stick to the bluff. "I'm not really following you on all this stuff about last night," he said carefully. "But, just hypothetically, are you saying that if someone broke into your business last night but didn't take anything, and if that someone chased off a couple guys who *were* trying to steal something—you're saying you'd offer that someone a job? And invite him to stay in the clinic overnight, legit?"

"Not just any someone," she said levelly. "But I have good instincts about people. And someone who cares enough about his dog to break in and hang out with him, and then cares enough about the clinic to challenge two intruders? That's the kind of person I'd want to trust with a job like this."

His panic was starting to change into something else, maybe something even more dangerous. "I have a criminal record," he told her. "I can't get hired at McDonalds with a record, and you want to trust me with this?"

"What's your record for?"

"A few things," he told her. Damn, she was asking him this *now*? She'd teased him with all her "good instincts" bullshit, make him start almost believing her, and now she was going to yank it all away. Damn her. But she'd find out about his record anyway, so there was no point in lying about it. "Disorderly conduct. Possession with intent. Resisting arrest."

"Possession?" she asked mildly. "Are you currently using drugs? Any addiction issues?"

"No. I mean, I'm not, like—what do you mean by 'currently'?"

"Grass and alcohol are legal now; I'm not asking if you ever smoke a joint or take a drink. But do you have a drug problem that would get in the way of your ability to do the job I'm suggesting?"

"No," he said. It was true; he'd take just about any drug anyone offered to him, but he wasn't addicted to any of them, and didn't even enjoy them that much. He just didn't like turning down free stuff that other people seemed to really value.

"If you take this job, will you do it to the best of your abilities?" she asked, and she looked him straight in the eye.

She wasn't judging him, he realized; she was giving him the chance to judge her. So he did his best. He looked back at her, tried to read her intentions, her attitude, or anything else that would be even a little bit useful to him, but he came up blank. Maybe if he was better at figuring people out he wouldn't get into trouble so often. As it was, though, he just found himself thinking of Dodger. She'd been gentle with the pup, and she'd taken care of him even knowing that it was going to be hard to get paid for her efforts.

"Yeah, I will," he said. It was a mistake, but he couldn't help himself. "I'll do the best I can."

"Okay." She smiled and nodded toward the door. "I need to get back to work, but if you decide you want to take the job, let me know and I'll get Noah to help you load the car."

"Yes," he said, too loudly for the small room. She was already past him, heading out, but she turned and raised an eyebrow. "If you're sure," he said, his voice more controlled. "Then, yes. I want the job."

"You're hired," she said easily. "If you stack the boxes in

the alley, I'll bring the car around when I've got a minute and you can load it up. We've got an air mattress at home; I can get my wife to bring it over this afternoon, and it'll do for a day or two, until I have time to get something better?"

"It'll do forever, really. I'm not picky."

"Deal was for a bed," she said firmly. "I'll keep the deal. Just give me a couple days."

And with that, she was gone, off to rescue kittens and heal puppies, or whatever else she did with her day. Shane stayed behind, looking around the little room in a bit of a daze. It seemed too good to be true, and his inner uncle was absolutely screaming at him, telling him to stay alert and look for the trap, or, barring that, the opportunity to take advantage of the situation.

The voice was probably right, and Shane knew it. So he'd keep his eyes open and try to figure it all out. But while he was waiting, and watching?

He stood in the middle of the room and stretched his arms out, then turned around. Once the boxes were gone, it would be a pretty okay space. It would be his, at least temporarily. Damn. While he was waiting and watching, he was going to be enjoying, as well.

Feral

Chapter Four

THERE WAS SOMETHING WEIRD going on with Dodger's hot owner.

Shit, no, just Dodger's owner. Nobody was hot. Noah wasn't noticing that, not at all. He was just trying to figure out what the 'weird' was.

Okay, maybe he'd noticed the guy's forearms after he'd pushed up the sleeves of his sweatshirt. They were strong-looking, that was all, not terribly thick but bulging and stretching in interesting ways as the guy carried box after box out of the storeroom and back to the alley. There were two bracelets on his left wrist, one smooth plastic, the other a band of braided cloth, and their delicacy somehow underscored the strength of the muscles they encircled. But mostly Noah was watching the boxes, trying to solve the mystery. The forearms were just a piece of the puzzle. The bruise on his face that hadn't been there the day before, right in that perfect spot where movie stars got a smudge of dirt in order to accentuate their cheekbones? This bruise was real, and it was another piece of the puzzle, almost certainly. And the guy's ass when he bent over to rearrange a few boxes? That was evidence of something, too, Noah was sure. Possibly evidence that a benevolent god existed and was smiling down on Seattle that day.

"Hi, Noah!" a female voice called, and he jerked his gaze away from the hot guy's ass to see Lena striding down the alley toward him. Lena, Dr. Anderson's wife, strode pretty much everywhere she went, her trademark cowboy boots practically striking sparks when they hit the pavement. She stopped in front of the hot guy and held out her hand. "And you must be Shane?"

Shane. Good to have a name for him. The guy took a moment to respond, which Noah could sympathize with. He always felt a bit slow around Lena, too, a bit behind the times, low on energy, and just overall dim. But Shane finally pulled himself together, wiped his hand on the leg of his baggy jeans, and then shook Lena's. "Yeah, hi," he said. "Do I know you?"

"Lena Cho. Tori's wife."

"Tori?"

"Dr. Anderson," Noah clarified, stepping into the conversation. "This is Dr. Anderson's wife." And then he braced himself. Most people were socialized well enough to not say anything overt about a same-sex couple, but this guy, with his neck tattoo and scowling face, clearly hadn't adopted the same rules that other people had. If he was going to be a homophobe, it was good that Noah was there to—well, to do nothing, probably, since he didn't want the shit kicked out of him. But at least he could sympathize with Lena afterward.

But the hot guy—Shane—didn't say anything inappropriate. He just nodded at the long canvas bag Lena was carrying in her free hand. "Is that for me?" he asked.

Lena beamed at him. "It is. There's a battery pump in there to blow it up, and I packed the set of sheets we usually use with it, too. They're a bit ratty, because, you know, camping, but they're the only double sheets we've got, so they'll have to do until we get something better, right?"

Noah's mind spun uselessly. Hot Shane was—going camping?

"They'll be fine," Shane said. "I don't need anything better."

"You're going to clean the room before you settle into it, right?" Lena looked as if she was ready to do a little scrubbing herself, and Noah finally put some pieces together. The boxes were out, the storage room was going to be clean, and for some unknown reason, Shane was going to be sleeping in it.

"Yeah, I can clean it," Shane said.

Noah wanted to ask some questions, even though he supposed none of it was any of his business, but then Lena turned to him and said, "And it's good that you're here, too! I wanted to talk to you both, if that's okay. I've got a project, and I'm hoping you guys can help me with it."

Shane looked immediately suspicious, but Noah had been involved in a couple of Lena's projects before, and they were generally pretty benign. "She's a social worker," he told Shane.

"She does things to help people."

The suspicion turned to something else, something even less pleasant. "I don't need help from a social worker," Shane growled.

"No, it's not about helping *you*," Lena said with a gentle laugh. "I want to *hire* you. Both of you, if you're interested. And then you'd be the ones helping other people."

"You want to hire me," Shane said, sarcasm making his voice almost a sneer. "Yeah, that makes sense. Because of all my work experience and valuable skills."

"Because of your experience, yes," Lena said as if she were oblivious to his tone. She smiled. "Just hear me out. Don't go getting all defensive before I've even explained the project, okay? If you listen to me and decide you're not interested, that's fine. I mean, it'll be a pain in the ass, because from what Tori's told me, you'd be great for the job, but it's your call. And it doesn't affect the deal you've made with Tori, one way or the other." She turned to Noah. "Same for you, of course. I mean, if you take this job, you probably won't have as much time to volunteer here anymore, but Tori says that's okay. But if you want to stay here, that's fine too. Your decision."

Noah looked at Shane. "They're like this," he said. "They're planners. I've still got another year of undergrad before I even *go* to vet school, but Dr. Anderson is already thinking about courses I should take and projects I should do while I'm studying.

They like to run things. But they're good about taking no for an answer, eventually."

Shane looked doubtful, but not of Noah, necessarily. It actually felt sort of like Shane and Noah were on the same side of whatever this was, and it probably wasn't good just how much Noah liked that feeling.

"So, what's the project?" Shane asked.

"I'm glad you asked." And Lena did sound genuinely happy about it. She looked at Noah, then at the boxes. "Can I help you guys tidy these up, and then we can go across the street and I'll buy you coffee and tell you all about it?"

Noah agreed readily, Shane more cautiously, and it only took a couple minutes to load the boxes with all three working at it. Noah tried not to let himself be distracted by the beauty of Shane's body, lifting, twisting, stretching, every movement a testament to the guy's strength and grace. It was even harder to avoid the seduction of simple comradeship, the way Shane moved quickly when he saw that Noah was having trouble with a box, catching the far corners and helping to balance it without comment or judgement. Noah wasn't sure if he was horny or just lonely. Most likely a pathetic combination of the two.

When the car was loaded, Lena bounced along between them as they walked out of the alley and across the street, and Noah had a strange moment of feeling like he was walking two dogs, a grumpy Rottweiler and a playful Golden Retriever puppy. Kind of weird that the puppy was pushing forty while the

Rottweiler might not even be twenty yet, but he figured personality counted more than age.

"So, this is something Tori and I have been working on for a long time," Lena said once they'd settled at a table. Noah tried to pay attention to her but he was a little distracted by watching Shane load sugar and cream into his mug of coffee. Five sugars and three creams. No, after a sip to bring the level down, *four* creams. It was like the guy was trying to turn the cup of coffee into a meal. "For a *long* time," Lena repeated, and she waited until Noah looked back toward her.

Then she smiled happily. "And now it seems like everything is finally coming together. The space next door has become available so we won't even have to move the clinic, we've made a lot of contacts and put together a list of volunteers, and we've got a line on a philanthropist who loves animals *and* supports a lot of anti-poverty work. It's perfect, really."

"What's perfect?" Shane asked, still sounding guarded.

"Okay, let me lay it out for you. I work with disadvantaged people, many of whom are homeless or living in substandard housing. Tori works with animals, and knows that a lot of people don't get their animals the care they need because of money problems. She's been taking care of that on an as-needed basis for years, offering payment plans or deferring payment or donating her time and finding charities that are willing to pay for medications. But she also takes paying customers because, let's face it, she needs to keep the clinic running and pay salaries."

Noah could feel Shane drawing back. It was too close to home, obviously, and why the hell couldn't Lena see that?

But maybe she could, because she kept speaking, a little more quickly, now. "Nobody's fault in any direction when people can't pay. Just the way of the world, and she's doing what she can to deal with it and help the animals. And obviously my focus is more on helping people. But the thing is, there are quite a few social programs out there for homeless people, quite a few ways for them to get off the streets, at least temporarily, and work toward a more secure life. At the very least, we have ways to get them some basic medical attention, or other vital services. And a lot of them take advantage of the programs, but quite a few don't. A surprising number, really. They need help, but they don't want to *take* help, at least not from us." She cut a quick look toward Shane, who was adding another damn sugar packet to his coffee. Noah wondered if the services Lena was talking about included dentistry, because there was no way the guy could like sugar that much and not have some cavity issues.

"So the plan," Lena said, "is to find a new way to reach these hard-to-serve people, or at least some of them." She finally looked at Noah, as if she had given up on Shane and was just hoping *someone* at the table would share her enthusiasm. "We need to find an entry point, a tool to build relationships with them and make them believe we're on their side. Too many have had bad experiences with some part of the system, and they don't trust any other part as a result. But we think we can reach the ones who have pets by offering services for the animals. Legitimate services," she added quickly. "Tori will supervise, and we've got other vets willing to volunteer some time, and technicians too. And we're talking to the vet school out in Pullman, and the colleges that offer technician training, to see if we can get students doing internships with us for course credit. We can offer immunizations, treatment for whatever the animals need, all at a discount rate or even free. So we can raise some money from animal lovers, for sure. And that's the side of the program that Tori's really excited about. But for me? For me, the great thing is that we'll get access to the pet owners. We're calling it the Dearborn Partnership—the street name, obviously, and then "partnership" as a salute to the people helping with it, but also to the people who will come to it. We'll build relationships, establish trust, and get an idea of what the clients need and how they can be best helped. So we'll have the Partnership clinic set up next door to Tori's clinic, connected, even, and the more serious cases can be treated in her facility. But in the other office, we'll have veterinary staff *and* social workers. So when people come in with their animals, we can talk to them and figure out how to help the people as well as the animals."

"You think people aren't going to see through that?" Shane asked. He didn't sound angry, exactly, but something close to it.

Lena wasn't intimidated, though, which made her a hell of a lot braver than Noah. "Some will. And some will walk because of it. Some will see through the plan, stick around for their pets, and then leave and not let us help them. But some of them?" Her eyes were shining now, her whole body almost glowing with the energy of true belief. "Some of them will let us help. Either because they don't see through the plan, or because they do but are willing to let us help anyway. Because they can use the animals as a way to get past their pride, or their resentment, or whatever else. You're right, the program won't work for everyone. But it will work for *some* people. And that makes it worthwhile, to me."

"And how do Shane and I fit into it?" Noah asked, trying to ignore the illicit, dangerous thrill of saying 'Shane and I' as if they were members of the same group. God, he needed to pull himself together. Did he need a friend that badly? He was too old for that nonsense, and damn it, he'd learned his lesson about trusting too quickly. He knew better.

"You and Shane are our recruiters," Lena said triumphantly. "Noah, you know enough about veterinary medicine to at least talk a good game and convince people their pets could use help. And Shane?" She looked over at him and raised her eyebrows. "He's your bodyguard, and your guide. He's the one who keeps your lilywhite ass from getting kicked all over The Jungle." She smiled as if it was cute to talk about visiting the notorious slopes where homeless people and crime were everywhere.

It took a moment to realize that she was serious. Okay, sure, Seattle was a safe city. But it was still a city, still had crime, and dangerous people, and—"The Jungle?" Noah said. Squeaked, maybe.

"Or wherever else you can find people who need help,"

Lena said. "Shane, I've got some ideas on that, and my colleagues and I will definitely refer people as we come across them, but there are people I just can't get to. And I think maybe you can."

That's what this was all about, Noah realized. His limited veterinary knowledge? It might be a little bit useful. His nonthreatening image? Maybe useful as well. But this was really about Shane.

Because he *was* perfect for the job. It was almost overwhelming, that epiphany. Noah felt as if he'd taken a step out of childhood and into a world where serious decisions were made, where people were observed and assessed and slotted into roles. Lena and Tori were kind, but they weren't stupid. They saw Shane for what he was, and what he could do for their causes. A tough street kid who loved his puppy, and who could tell people about the vet who'd saved the little dog. Shane was their perfect tool, and for a moment Noah felt almost bitter, almost resentful, and all on Shane's behalf, which made no sense. If he had any loyalty in all this, surely it was toward Dr. Anderson, who'd been so supportive of him.

"You want me to talk people into taking their pets to your vet?" Shane asked. It was a relief to hear the cynicism in his voice; Noah didn't need to protect Shane, because Shane could take care of himself. "You want me to be a fucking salesman?"

"Kind of," Lena agreed easily. "No actual sales, though. I mean, we're not going to charge anyone for anything, not if they can't afford it."

"But you're going to milk some rich person for their money," Shane said.

Lena gave him another look, even as she was nodding her agreement. "That's what it comes down to, yes. This program is valuable, both Tori and I believe. But it only works if we can persuade other people that it's useful. And, yes, Mrs. Carson, the philanthropist we have in mind, needs to be persuaded." She stopped for a second, then shrugged and said, "Milked. We need to convince her to let us milk her."

"That's kind of gross," Noah said. He immediately wished he hadn't spoken. Shane and Lena were having some jaded, worldly, layered conversation, and he was spouting off about their figures of speech. He was a child in the company of adults and he should keep his damn mouth shut.

But Shane's lean face was twisted into something approaching a smirk, at least some of his earlier tension gone. "They have those machines they stick onto cows—"

"Okay, we are not going to discuss different methods of milking Mrs. Carson," Lena said firmly. "The point is, she's fairly hands-on, or at least feet-on—she'll want to tour the facility and see what we're doing. If we can show her a clinic full of people and pets, we've got a good chance of getting some serious funding. If the place is empty, or only has Tori's regular paying customers, Mrs. Carson won't be inspired to keep it going, right? So, we've got enough money for a good start-up and to keep things scraping along for quite a while. We've got funding from a few different agencies for the social workers who'll be on site. But if we can get Mrs. Carson's support, we can have a lot more security and really build something worthwhile."

Shane looked—well, it wasn't easy to say how he looked, really. The smirk was gone, but so was just about every other hint of an expression. His resting face was vaguely suspicious, vaguely hostile, but mostly just disinterested. "It doesn't sound like my thing," he said. "I'm not really into charity, or whatever."

"Are you into employment?" Lena asked. "Because this would be paid work. Just minimum wage, and probably only twenty hours a week, but with your accommodation taken care of you could live pretty well on that money and still have time for whatever else you do. And you'd be building a work history, something that would help future employers overlook the criminal record."

Shane still didn't look too enthusiastic, but Lena didn't let it slow her down. "Think about it," she said. "You don't need to make an instant decision or anything. And if you have any questions, you can ask Tori, or me." She looked at Noah. "If you're interested and Shane isn't, we'll have to—I'm not sure. We'll have to try to find someone else to work with you, I think, because it wouldn't be safe for you to go out on your own."

Maybe Noah was a coward, but he had no intention of challenging her decision about that. The job sounded intriguing, but intimidating, and he didn't want to take it on alone. But the thought of working with Shane? The two of them a team, facing danger together?

Like buddies in a cop movie. Thrown together by circumstances, kept together by trust. And by one cop's powerful desire to lick the other cop all over. Damn. He was back to it, the war between lust and loneliness. Either way, he knew better. The last time he'd trusted someone too quickly had ended with flashing lights and lawyers, humiliation and pain. He was on a good path now, working hard and meeting his goals. He needed to stay strong, stay disciplined.

Still, he found himself nodding. "Okay. I think I'd like to do it, but you're right—I shouldn't do it on my own. So it's up to Shane."

And just like that, the fragile rapport Noah had been building, or imaging, was gone. Shane shot him a dirty look, then turned back to Lena as if Noah was beneath his notice. "I'll get back to you," he said. "But you shouldn't hold your breath." With that, he gulped down the sweet, creamy mess in his mug and then pushed to his feet. "Thanks for the coffee."

He strode away then, leaving the café like he was a businessman on his way to an important meeting, and Noah stared after him. "Why's he mad?"

"He might not be, really," Lena said. "Sometimes that's just a safe default expression, you know?"

Noah *didn't* know. He didn't know a damn thing about Shane, or what had just happened in the conversation, or much of anything else. But he wanted to find out. Even though he should have known better.

Chapter Five

IT WAS STRANGE TO scrub the storage room, strange to think of making a place nicer for himself. For too long, Shane had lived in public or in other people's spaces; even when he'd been living with Uncle Davey, he'd been sharing space with lots of other kids.

This? He'd seen a mop in the closet that held cleaning supplies, but he'd grabbed a scrub brush instead, and he was down on his hands and knees, working hard enough that he was a little out of breath as he powered through layers of dirt on the old linoleum. And it felt good.

Part of that good feeling, of course, was just because he was able to at least partly distract himself from thinking about the stupid plan for the clinic. Or maybe the plan itself wasn't stupid; yeah, if he was being honest, the general idea was actually kind of interesting. It was the idea of him being part of it that made no sense.

Well, maybe it kind of made sense, from the outside. If someone didn't know him, didn't know he was a screw-up who trusted the wrong people and got in fights all the time and didn't have any goddamn sense at all, then maybe they'd think he'd be okay for the job. That Lena, she was a social worker, and he knew enough about social workers to know that they didn't always see the world the way it was. Lots of big ideas, that's what social workers had, but that didn't mean they knew anything about actually turning their ideas into reality.

Shit, maybe he needed something a bit better to distract himself with; the scrubbing didn't seem to be doing the trick.

Still, he managed to keep his mind more-or-less on the job until he finished the floor and then used the mop to give it a final rinse. Hell, yeah. This was his space. Not forever, he was sure, but even if he only got to sleep in it for a couple nights, that made the cleaning worthwhile.

And that was all he should look for, he knew. Dodger was getting better, and they both had a safe, warm, dry place to sleep. That was two really, really good things. Pushing for more? Trying to come out of all this with a damn job on top of everything else? It was tempting fate, for sure.

So he put the cleaning supplies back in the closet and left the door to his room—*his room*—open so it could get some air and dry out, and then he went down the hall to the room with the cages.

The preppy boy was in there. Noah. Shane was tempted to back out before he was noticed, but damn it, he wasn't going to start being scared off by skinny, Gap-wearing nerds. So he made himself continue into the room, and when Noah smiled at him, he managed to not frown back.

"Dr. Anderson says you can take him out of the cage," Noah announced. He sounded genuinely excited. "She says he has to take it easy, and we'll keep monitoring him, but he's responding really well to the treatment. No more IVs or anything, so he may as well be with you."

Shane stared at him. "Seriously? Like, I can take him out and not put him back in?"

Noah nodded, and this time when he smiled, Shane almost smiled back. Instead, he crossed the room and lifted his hand up to the latch of the cage.

Something was going to go wrong. The latch would be stuck, or Shane would reach inside and feel something wet and pull his hand back and find it covered in blood, or—something else horrible would happen. One way or another, Shane would have to pay for the good things people were offering to him, and since the only thing he actually had to lose was Dodger... He swallowed hard, squeezed the latch, and let the door swing open on well-oiled hinges.

And then he moved fast, because *Dodger* was moving fast, launching himself out of the cage, never mind that it was at Shane's shoulder-height. It wasn't all that hard to catch him, but it was pretty tricky to keep a grip on him as he wriggled and squirmed and yipped. He seemed to be alternating between trying to burrow into Shane's chest and trying to climb up on his head, doing both with full enthusiasm and a hell of a lot of extra shimmying.

Shane sank to the floor where at least the fall would be less serious if he couldn't hold on and where his crossed legs gave a sort of platform for Dodger's hind limbs. "Shhhh," he said desperately. "You're supposed to be taking it easy. Settle down, Dodge. Chill out. It's okay, buddy, you're free. No more cage, okay?"

"He's been out of the cage a few times before, when we were treating him," Noah said quietly. Shane had almost forgotten the guy was in the room. "And he never acted like this. I'm sure he didn't like the cage, and I'm sure he's feeling better and has more energy. But he's not acting like this just because he's out of the cage. He's happy because he's with you."

They were just words. It wasn't like Noah was some sort of animal emotions expert, or anyone else who knew anything about anything. But still, Dodger did seem really happy, and Shane buried his face in the puppy's warm fur. "No more cage," he said again, his voice muffled.

He gave himself a moment to just savor the pup's warmth. Not cold and dead, not this dog. He would have been, though. Shane looked up to see Noah looking down at him, a strange expression on his face. "He almost died," Shane said. Partly defensiveness, but partly—what? Partly an invitation to share the celebration, maybe. A miracle had occurred, and Shane shouldn't be the only witness.

But Noah shrugged. "If he hadn't made it here, I guess it might have been bad. But once Dr. Anderson got hold of him? She's really good at her job, you know."

Shane looked down at Dodger. The pup's burst of enthusiasm seemed to have tired him out, and he was snuggling into Shane's lap, now, his eyes already closing in contentment. Dodger was alive because Shane had found Dr. Anderson. Two other veterinary clinics had taken one look at Shane and then asked for pre-payment, and turned him away when he couldn't provide. But one of the people at the second place had jogged after him, out into the rain, and suggested he try Dr. Anderson's clinic.

Shane could do that, he realized. He could be the one making the suggestions, helping people find ways to take care of their pets. He pictured himself standing in the rain, soaked and cold, handing out sodden flyers. It was somehow easier to accept it as a possibility if he focused on the negative parts of it. He generally kept to himself, or talked only to people he already knew. Going out and trying to meet strangers? He wouldn't like that. And it could even be dangerous, considering some of the crazies out there. Sure, he was a good size, and he was quick and tough, but the problem with crazies was they couldn't be predicted. So, yeah, he'd have to keep an eye out for knives, or worse, and he'd have to look after Noah, too. And Dodger. Shit, he'd have to do all this while making sure Dodger wasn't eating anything bad again, or wasn't stepping on sharp things or getting bullied by other dogs, or whatever else might happen.

This job would really suck.

His shoulders had relaxed some as he'd hunched over Dodger, welcoming the little guy back to the land of the living, and now he felt them soften a little more. The job was crap. It wasn't tempting fate for him to take a crappy job, it was just life. *His* life. Some people might get to work inside, or drive around in a nice car, or get free food or—well, his imagination wasn't really good enough to figure out any more perks that some people might have at their jobs. But he knew he wouldn't be getting any of them. If he took this job, helping other Dodgers get the help they needed, he'd have a miserable time, and he wouldn't make much money, and he'd probably end up with the crap beat out of him or catching his death of cold.

No wonder the social worker had offered it to him; nobody with any sense would want to do it.

He looked up at Noah. "You think I could still take that job? The one with you, going around and finding people? You think it's too late for me to talk to her about it?"

"It's been, like, an hour and a half. I really don't think she'll have changed her mind in an hour and a half."

"People are weird sometimes," Shane said defensively. Having a reasonable boss didn't really fit into his vision of future employment; everything would be much easier to accept if he could believe she was going to be difficult. "Maybe I'd better go see if I can find her."

"Yeah, okay," Noah said. He sounded a bit unsure, and that was good, too. Shane had to work with a stuck-up preppy who didn't understand simple conversations and was afraid to talk to homeless people without a bodyguard. So annoying.

"You want me to watch Dodger while you go find her?" Noah volunteered.

Stupid suck-up, thinking he could steal Shane's dog? Shane pushed himself to his feet, drowsy Dodger held in the crook of his arm. He felt good. Light, somehow, like Dodger was the reverse of a weight, and carrying him made Shane float. "Keep your paws off my helium dog," he told Noah. "You want one, go find your own."

"Your *helium* dog?" Noah said, but Shane was already out of the room.

He had a mission. A crappy job to accept and suffer through. "It's gonna suck, right Dodge?" he asked, and he held the puppy up a little higher to allow a chin lick. "But maybe we'll be able to help some people. Some dogs. Hell, maybe we'll even help some cats. Maybe."

He found Lena in the tiny office behind the front desk. "Job still open?" he asked.

She didn't even look up from the papers she was reading over. "When can you start?"

"My time is flexible," he told her, and he resisted the urge to smile.

*****

It was strange, sitting there in the café with Lena and Dr. Anderson and Shane. Strange at least partly because Noah was the only one who seemed to think anything unusual was going on. Like they were the sort of people who usually hit the spot together for a late Saturday lunch: two professional women, a slightly nerdy young man, and a gorgeous thug sneaking nibbles of his burger to the puppy hidden inside his hoodie.

"Tiny bits of people food are okay to tempt his appetite," Dr. Anderson warned. "But he needs to mostly be eating the dog food I gave you. That's what will get him strong fastest."

Shane nodded seriously. "It just seems rude to eat a whole meal and not give him any."

"You think he's going to share his kibble with you tonight?"

"He would if I asked, yeah."

That shut Dr. Anderson up, which wasn't something Noah saw every day, and he let himself savor the occasion for just a moment before turning his mind back to business.

They'd already talked about the details of the clinic: now that the space next door was available, the social workers were ready to move in, and the veterinary functions would be easily blended in with the existing clinic operations. The more clients they could attract, the more funding they'd be able to apply for, so the growth of the project depended pretty seriously on getting the word out to the relevant communities.

And despite Lena's contacts, Noah and Shane were going to be important to that last part.

"You're looking at everyone who can't afford a vet, right?" Shane asked. He'd been quiet when they'd first sat down, but he was loosening up, now. "Like, not just people who need social workers or health care or whatever. This is about the animals as much as the people?"

Lena nodded cautiously, Dr. Anderson more emphatically.

"So we're going to have to go to a lot of different places at different times. There's the tents and whatever in the Jungle, and some other places too. Probably best to go there in the late morning."

"The morning?" Lena asked. "I'm not questioning your expertise, but can you explain?"

Shane gave her a suspicious look, like he thought maybe she was making fun of him, but when she kept her expression calm, he said, "If you go earlier than that, you'll be waking people up, and they won't be happy. If you go later, they might already be too drunk or stoned or whatever, and that could get messy. You don't want to go after dark—" He looked at Noah, then back at Lena, and said, "There's some places that'll be better at night, but I should probably hit them alone, if that works for you. I can take some flyers or something, to fill in for what I don't know about the actual vet stuff."

That stung a little. Noah's passion and knowledge was going to be replaced by a flyer? But he probably didn't want to argue based on hurt feelings. Instead, he said, "Is it safe for you to be going those places alone? I mean, why don't you want me to come?"

Shane just raised an eyebrow and gave Noah the slightest version of a once over, making it clear that he'd already made his assessment and was just looking to be sure nothing had changed. It was just that little bit of extra dismissal when Dodger peeked out from his spot inside Shane's hoodie, gave Noah a sleepy look, then ducked back inside as if he'd found nothing interesting. Shane said, "There's some people who will want to talk to you. And there's some people who won't. Most of the ones who won't are around at night."

"But they'll want to talk to you?"

"They're my friends. Or friends of friends, or they'll know me from somewhere, or at least I'll look like they expect people to look. I won't have to worry about getting my clothes dirty."

It somehow hadn't occurred to Noah that Shane would have friends. Maybe because Noah had so few himself. But he didn't have friends because he was busy, with work and school and family. Shane didn't have any of those distractions, so maybe he just hung out with people all day long. Getting dirty. "I don't know much about you," Noah said quietly. "I get that. But you don't know much about me, either, okay? So, first thing you can learn is: I'm not too worried about dirty clothes."

There was a moment of stillness at the table. Not quite tension, just a sort of waiting. Lena and Dr. Anderson, watching to see if they needed to step in. Noah, remembering too late his earlier trepidation about Shane, wondering if he'd gone too far. And Shane, sitting quietly, dark eyes focused on Noah as if they were reading his soul. It felt like forever but was probably only a couple seconds before Shane said, "That's not the first thing I've learned about you. If it was, I wouldn't be here." Then, as if he hadn't just dropped a cryptic comment that would have Noah pondering for ages, he told the women, "It doesn't have to be paid time. I can just take some flyers with me when I see people. They're going to want to know what I'm doing, so I can tell them."

"Networking," Lena said with satisfaction. "That's the name of the game."

And it was the area where Noah wasn't going to be much use. Shane had been the one who'd said it, but neither Lena nor Dr. Anderson had disagreed.

It was a continual adjustment to his mindset, Noah realized. He knew better, but he kept slipping into considering himself the leader, with Shane added into the mix mostly as a charitable act, a way to get him some money despite his pride. But in reality, the situation was reversed. Shane was perfect for the job, and Noah was the extra, the tag-along. Apparently his ego made that a bit hard to accept.

He looked up from the scratched melamine table top to find that Shane was still watching him. "Do you want to start tomorrow?" Shane asked. His voice wasn't quite deferential, but it was careful, as if he knew Noah was struggling with something and didn't want to add to it.

"Tomorrow's Sunday," Noah said.

"Do you have to go to church or something?"

"No, I don't have to go to church. But—" But what? What was he worried about? "The clinic isn't open on Sundays, and the social workers are only planning to be there on weekdays. What's the point of getting people excited about a place that they can't use until later?"

"People are going to have to think about it," Shane said immediately. "Not if there's an emergency," and he unconsciously cradled the Dodger-shaped bulge in his hoodie, "but if you're thinking about rabies shots or whatever? People aren't going to come down for that until they're sure it's a good idea. I know a few people with pets; I can get them to come in first, even if there's nothing wrong with the animals. You said you'd do rats and ferrets and stuff, not just dogs and cats, right?"

"Anything that gets people into the clinic," Lena said confidently.

"We don't have an exotic pet expert, not full time," Dr. Anderson said more cautiously. "I've got a few contacts who are willing to help out, but they'll need to be booked ahead of time, not available for drop-ins."

Shane nodded. "It's going to be slow going at the start. Anything new, people aren't crazy about, and—" He gave both women a look as if deciding how much to say. "They won't trust social workers, not a lot of them. Too many have been burned by the system already. And, a lot of them—they aren't going to be crazy about vet stuff, either. They don't want to end up with autistic dogs from vaccinations or whatever. It's going to take a while to get them to trust you."

"But less time to get them to trust *you*," Lena said. She sounded almost smug, clearly pleased with her plan. "And you can take Dodger with you as evidence, right?"

"Wrong," Dr. Anderson said. "Dodger's still recovering. He's doing well, and he needs to get some light exercise, absolutely. He shouldn't spend the rest of his life in your shirt. But he was too young to be vaccinated before you found him, and we don't really have any reason to believe his mom was vaccinated, either, if she was owned by the kind of assholes who discard puppies like garbage. We'll give him his shots as soon as he's healthy, but until then I don't want him around unvaccinated dogs."

Lena frowned at her, but didn't say anything. Noah had the feeling there was going to be a domestic discussion about the issue later, but it was pretty hard to argue with the general principle. Dodger would be a great sales tool as long as he was healthy, but he needed to be kept safe.

Noah glanced at Shane and realized that he was waiting for something. Waiting—oh, shit. "But you still want Shane, even if Dodger can't go with him, right?" Noah said quickly. "Dodger will be useful eventually, but Shane's still got lots to do in the meantime. Right?"

Lena's frown disappeared, replaced by a look of surprised contrition. "Oh, yeah, Shane, of course! It's your job, and you're going to be great at it. It's not about Dodger—I was just getting ahead of myself, being a bit too clever. Nothing to worry about."

She sounded calm and confident, as usual, and Shane nodded his understanding. But there was something different about him. One careless idea, quickly retracted, had been enough to send him back to being the guy he'd been the day before when he'd first brought Dodger in. Cautious, maybe even suspicious.

That was okay, Noah told himself. For one thing, it wasn't any of Noah's business if some random hot guy was comfortable in his new job. For another—well, for another, Noah was pretty sure this new state was temporary. "We should start tomorrow," he said into the silence. "Absolutely." He didn't need to do his homework or anything, did he? No, he'd be fine.

And he was rewarded when he saw Shane nod and seem just a little more confident than he had a moment before. There was another strange moment of feeling like he and Shane were

on the same team, and this time instead of dismissing it, Noah let himself enjoy it. It was just an illusion, but it was a nice one.

Chapter Six

AFTER LUNCH, NOAH AND the women went back to the clinic, while Shane took Dodger down the street to a little park. Not much space, but Dr. Anderson had said she'd never seen other dogs using it, which meant it was reasonably safe for the unimmunized pup. And there was enough room for him to walk around a little, and for Shane to stare at him like the miracle he was. Still a bit wobbly, and Dr. Anderson had made it clear that he shouldn't be allowed to tire himself out, but he was sniffing and exploring and even managed to chase after a dead leaf for a few strides.

They stayed there for quite a while. Shane thought about tracking some people down and letting them know what he was up to, but it wasn't important right then. He'd go over to Tristan's at some point and pick up his knapsack full of stuff, but he was in no hurry. Tristan was too social, too generous with his space, which meant there was always a crowd in his small apartment. And for all Shane's talk about getting his friends involved in the project, he wasn't quite ready to explain the situation to any of them. They'd be suspicious, as they damn well should be—as *he* should be—and he didn't want to answer any hard questions yet. He just wanted to enjoy the hopefulness for a little longer before people started pointing out all the problems with it. Like holding onto a lottery ticket instead of checking it, because until it was proved to be a loser, there was still always at least a tiny chance it had won.

The park was overgrown, maybe more of a vacant lot than a real park, and Shane liked that. He found a spot near the corner where he could stand still and be practically invisible from the street, hidden behind the shrubs. But he could see everything all the way down to the clinic, and he watched the place for a while. Like a predator stalking its prey, maybe, except he was pretty sure he wasn't the predator in this situation. So maybe like prey watching a predator, but did it really make any sense for prey to sit around and watch instead of just getting the hell away?

Maybe he was a mix, he figured. There'd been cats in some of the houses he'd lived in when he was a kid, and he'd always found them kind of intriguing. They were hunters, sure, but they got chased, too. Lots of animals wanted to eat them—dogs, coyotes, wild cats—probably more than that, really. So cats had to walk a pretty fine line. They had to be bold enough to be good hunters, but shy enough to make sure they didn't get eaten. It probably wasn't too weird that cats spent so much of their time hiding and watching, Shane decided as he peered out from the shrubs.

He saw Noah coming down the street toward him, and watched the way the guy moved. Not like a cat, that was for sure. Totally clueless, really, not even noticing the potential threats on all sides. The guy sitting on the steps watching him, sizing him up, deciding if he was carrying enough cash to be worth the trouble of robbing? Maybe Noah wasn't used to people like that and didn't know he needed to keep an eye on them. And the drunk stumbling toward him who could be carrying a knife, could so easily change a stumble into a lunge, and then a stabbing? He probably *was* just drunk, and it was only Shane's paranoia thinking Noah should have taken a step to the side as they passed. But the guy in the beat-up navy pickup who took the corner too fast and then weaved for a bit as he regained control? There were crazy drivers in every neighborhood, so it wasn't a sign of Noah coming from somewhere better that made him clueless on that one. He just wasn't careful enough, and Shane wasn't sure how to feel about that. Maybe it was kind of good, kind of nice for Noah, at least, to be able to wander through life as if it was just a ride at an amusement park.

Shane stepped out of the shrubs before Noah got too close; no need to look like a stalker, not that Noah was likely to even notice. Dodger was back inside Shane's sweatshirt, having a nap, but he poked his head out to see what was going on when Shane said, "Hey. You looking for us?"

"Actually, yeah. Both of you." Noah held out a small blue collar with a thin leash attached. "They have a bunch of extras at the clinic, and I was cleaning out the cupboard where they keep them, and I thought maybe you and Dodger would like to have one?"

"I can buy him a leash," Shane said, looking down at the length of cord he'd been using. Stupid to have forgotten about that. And, sure, maybe he was a bit short of cash, but what he couldn't buy, he'd get some other way. Some way that *didn't* involve taking handouts.

"Okay," Noah said. "Do you want it as a loaner, until you get around to it? That's what they're for, you know. People come in and their leashes are messed up or something, so we loan one to them. Same with the collars. If you don't like this color, you could look for a different one."

Shane honestly couldn't tell whether the guy was playing him, and that was a bit disturbing. It wasn't like Noah was some sort of master con artist or anything. Not unless he was running a deep, *deep* game. "The color's fine. I just—"

Dodger was watching the whole thing with interest, and he deserved to have a nice, matching leash and color instead of a chunk of rope. He'd look good in blue. "Maybe just a loan," Shane said. Then he forced out a "Thanks."

"There's shampoo and stuff, too, when he's feeling a bit stronger. If you wanted to give him a bath."

"You saying my dog stinks?"

Noah just shrugged. "A bath wouldn't hurt. Once he's strong enough."

And that was that. The guy smiled, handed over the leash, and headed back to the clinic, and after a few more minutes in the park, Shane followed. Everyone was busy, closing up for the day, and Dr. Anderson gave him a quick rundown on the animals who were staying overnight. There would be a vet tech coming in to check on things, just as there had been the night before, but Shane could keep an eye on them between times.

It was enough responsibility to make his skin crawl, but not quite enough to make him run away. It wasn't like he was there *instead* of the vet tech, he reminded himself. He wasn't replacing the help the animals would have had without him, so it wasn't like he could make things worse for them. So it was okay; he couldn't mess it up too bad.

He frowned at the little card attached to each cage and tried to remember all of Dr. Anderson's explanations. "Shit," he muttered.

"My first job with an animal here was trimming a cat's nails," a newly familiar voice said from behind him. Shane jumped a little, then turned around and tried to figure out what the hell Noah was talking about. Noah smiled ruefully. "I went too short on one of them, and drew a little blood. Not a big deal, but the cat freaked out and I lost my grip and she took off, and I hadn't shut the door of the exam room because—I don't know, I guess because it was a small exam room and there just wasn't much space with me and the cat and the tech—so the cat was loose, and she went racing through the clinic, leaving bloody footprints as she went, and she charged right out to the front room where her owner was waiting. And the owner freaked out, obviously, and the cat was still freaked and she went bouncing up the wall of the display shelf and almost fell off and then just sat up there bleeding and hissing when we got close, and the owner was screaming at me the whole time, and she was totally justified. I messed up. It was a simple job, but I messed it up, and the cat suffered because of it, and the owner was traumatized, and—" He stopped talking and shook his head. "It was pretty terrible."

"Was that supposed to be a fucking pep talk?" Shane demanded. "You think anything about that story is going to make me *relax* about tonight?"

Noah snorted a rough laugh. "Yeah, I started rethinking it half-way through. Sorry. But the reason I thought it might help was that, you know—I'm still here. Dr. Anderson didn't fire me, and I didn't curl up in a ball and give up, and the cat was fine, and the owner—well, the owner's still pretty pissed, I think, and she's given orders that I'm not allowed to work on her cat anymore, but that's fair, really. So it was pretty bad, but I survived it. So even if something did go wrong tonight, which it won't, you'll survive it too. That was what I was trying to say."

At some point, Shane needed to figure out how Noah had even known Shane was feeling insecure, but he let that question go for right then. "I'm not even going to touch any animals besides Dodger. I'm definitely not going to cut anyone's toes off."

"I didn't cut it *off*! It was just a little nick! I'm not saying it didn't hurt, and I'm sorry it happened, but—"

"Noah, I was kidding." Shane watched as Noah tried to calm down. It was probably a bit mean, teasing the guy when he'd just been trying to help Shane out, but it didn't seem like any permanent harm had been done.

"Sorry," Noah said sheepishly. "I still feel pretty guilty about it."

"If that's the worst you've got to feel guilty about, I don't think you need to worry too much."

"It's not," Noah said. Then he caught himself, clearly realizing he didn't want the conversation to go in that direction. "So, anyway, the point was, you'll be fine. And if you want, I take the bus past here on my way home from work. I can come check in, probably around nine, if you want? The buses run every twenty minutes, so I could get off one bus, catch the next one, and it wouldn't be a big deal."

It was stupid to feel so relieved. Stupid to even think of accepting the offer. Shane wasn't a little kid, and it wasn't like he was afraid to be in the clinic alone. It was just the animals. He knew nothing, and he didn't make good decisions, and he'd really, really hate it if one of his mistakes hurt an innocent creature. He'd already let Dodger get sick. "You'll be tired, after working. You'll want to go right home."

"No, it's a pretty short shift. I just work the meal rushes—a few hours in the morning, a few hours at night. I don't get that tired." He shrugged. "And it'd be kind of cool to see the clinic after hours. You know, it'll let me pretend I'm already a vet and this is *my* practice."

"And you just happen to have some random guy sleeping in your storage room."

"I'm quirky that way."

"Let me check with Dr. Anderson. I know she doesn't want people hanging out in here after hours, but she'd probably make an exception for you."

"Okay," Noah agreed easily. "And if she's not okay with it, that's fine. You'll be totally okay on your own. Nothing bad is going to happen."

Well, that was just a lie, of course. Something bad was going to happen, sooner or later. Something bad *always* happened, sooner or later. The best Shane could hope for was *later*.

But being around Noah made it easier to forget that. The guy was a distraction, sure, but there was also something about him. He was just—hopeful? No, that wasn't the right word. Hopeful made it sound like there was some doubt. Noah was confident. He was doing his thing, studying or whatever, and that meant he was going to be a vet. He wasn't thinking about any of the stuff that could go wrong and get in his way, he was just getting shit done.

He was naïve, of course. He didn't know all the ways things could get messed up, but not knowing about them didn't mean they wouldn't happen all the same.

But at least for now, Noah seemed pretty happy with his plans, and it was kind of nice to be around someone like that. Shane had other optimistic friends, he supposed, but their dreams were less grounded than Noah's. Being sure your next trick was going to be a talent scout who'd take you to Hollywood wasn't really a plan for the future, it was a delusion. Noah's idea, though?

Noah's plan was something that would work, if the world was a fair and reasonable place. And Noah apparently thought the world *was* that kind of place, and it was—nice. Nice to be around someone who hadn't realized the world was shit.

So Shane went to find Dr. Anderson and he got permission for Noah's visit, and then he went back to his room and lay down on the air mattress, Dodger snuggled in beside him. He cradled the dog between his arm and his ribs and he looked up at the clean ceiling, and he let himself dream, just for a moment, about living in the world Noah believed in.

*****

Noah should have spent the afternoon studying. Exams were coming up and he needed to do well on them. He took the same pre-med courses as the students who wanted to be doctors, and the conventional wisdom was that he'd need higher marks to get into vet school than they'd need to get into med school.

He could sort of justify the part of the day that had been spent talking about the Dearborn Partnership. He wanted to be involved in the project because he believed in it and because it sounded interesting, but he was also totally aware that it would look good on his applications. Pretty much every prospective vet student would have volunteered in a clinic and gotten good grades, but something like the Dearborn Partnership was less common, and that would be useful. So, yeah, he could give himself the excuse if he wanted. But if he was being completely honest?

He sat there on the bus, travelling to his evening shift at the restaurant, and made himself admit it. He'd wanted to spend time with Shane. There was something intriguing about him, even beyond the physical appeal. But that was no excuse. Noah was doing it again, letting himself be distracted by a guy, and it was even worse this time because he wasn't a kid anymore and because he'd already had his warning. He knew better.

And it wasn't just the distraction, he reminded himself. Shane was—okay, he was physically impressive. The tattoo that had initially seemed ugly and dangerous had somehow changed. It still felt aggressive, maybe, but in a more artistic way. All day, Shane's hoodie had kept bunching up around his neck, blocking most of the ink, and Noah'd had to curl his fingers into fists to keep from reaching and pushing the fabric away. God, maybe he wouldn't just touch the fabric, maybe he'd let his fingertips brush against the skin itself, and Shane would suck in a breath of air, but he wouldn't move away. And fantasy Noah was a hell of a lot more confident than real Noah, so he'd flatten his hand against Shane's neck, slide it deeper under the sweatshirt, and he'd lean forward to admire the tattoo with his eyes, then his lips. His tongue.

He shifted uncomfortably on the molded plastic chair of the bus. Damn it. He needed to get his brain back on track. The tattoo was interesting, sure, and Shane's dark eyes, his golden-brown skin, his angular face with its strong jaw and high cheekbones—okay, all of it. All of it was interesting. Attractive. His tight ass and broad shoulders and strong arms. Shane was physically impressive. Impressive enough to beat the shit out of a suburban gay kid stupid enough to get handsy, and *that* was what Noah needed to be thinking about.

Sure, the guy hadn't seemed too alarmed by Lena and Dr. Anderson, but a lot of straight guys thought lesbians were hot. That was totally different than being approached themselves.

Not that Noah would ever have the nerve to actually make an approach anywhere but in his mind, of course, so all of this was completely hypothetical.

He climbed off the bus and ducked around the back of the restaurant, joining the other servers hanging around for the last possible moments of freedom before starting their shift. Carrie, a mother of two who sometimes seemed willing to be a mother of everyone, saw him coming and made an unhappy face at him. "I was inside already, dropping off my stuff. That guy's here again, with his friends."

Noah felt his entire body tense and tried to keep his face neutral. "Oh," he said. Roman, and his friends. "Did they—"

What? Did they seem any more or less sadistic than usual? "Did they seem like they'd been here for a while? Maybe they're almost done."

"They were just drinking," she said, clearly knowing she was bearing bad news. "Seemed like they were starting their night, not finishing their day."

Oh, good, drinking. That should make everything much more controlled and civilized. Noah's stomach was so tight he was pretty sure he wouldn't be lying if he told the manager he had to go home sick, but he thought of Sarah's damn zoo trip, and his tuition, and the scholarship he didn't have because of Roman—no, because of his own stupidity, but his stupidity *about* Roman—and he knew he had to go in.

"They're not in your section," Carrie said. "You can just ignore them."

She didn't sound like she believed it herself, and Noah certainly didn't. Roman didn't like to be ignored, and he was completely willing to do whatever it took to get someone's attention. When they'd been teenagers, his intensity had been fascinating, intoxicating. Noah had spent his whole life worrying about what people thought, and then he'd met Roman and it had been like finding a doorway to an exciting new world. Freedom and adventure and a total disregard for social conventions.

Now, of course, Noah would like it if a few more social conventions would apply. Like the one about not confronting an ex-boyfriend in public, at his place of work. Maybe one about letting things go, and not humiliating people who've already been hurt enough.

But that was the problem, of course. There was no *enough* for Roman, not until he got bored and decided to move on. Almost four years after their break-up, Roman still wasn't ready for that. His visits had become less frequent, maybe, his attention less pervasive than it had been at the start. But he still liked to check in on Noah every month or so, just to be sure he still had his power.

"We'd better get in there," Carrie said to the group, and they all reluctantly headed for the door.

Noah trailed in last. He'd changed into his black pants and white shirt before he left the clinic, so all he had to do was wash his hands, tie on an apron, and try to build up his courage.

Maybe Roman was just there for drinks or dinner, nothing to do with Noah. Yeah, sure, because a family-style restaurant in a damn strip mall was just the sort of place Roman would want to hang out.

Okay, different approach. Maybe this time, Noah would finally man up and tell Roman to fuck off. Yeah, he'd probably lose his job if he made a scene at work, but maybe it would be worth it. Of course, Roman wouldn't care if Noah made a fuss, wouldn't leave just because Noah told him to. He'd bask in the drama, the excitement, and probably come back more often if he got it.

So Noah was back to the "ignore him" strategy, even though it had never yet been effective.

It worked well enough for the first part of the shift, at least. Noah introduced himself to the few customers already seated at tables in the section he was taking over and was only vaguely aware of the boisterous crowd of young men sitting by the front windows. Of course Roman was in a crowd; he'd used to call them his entourage, and only been partly joking. He was beautiful and charismatic and damn it, he was fun, at least for a little while. Noah had been thrilled when he'd become part of the group, and even more excited when Roman began to single him out and give him a little more attention. Private, personal attention, although even when they'd been their most intimate, there had usually been only a thin door between them and the rest of the party.

Now? Noah didn't even let himself look in the direction of the long table filled with laughing young men. He was vaguely aware of them making dinner orders, and certainly grateful when Carrie recruited other servers to help carry the food out. But that was all.

At least, it was all until he was at the bar, waiting for a drinks order to be put together, and felt someone ease in beside him, too close to be casual. The servers were all fairly physical with each other—working in tight quarters made that efficient, and comfortable. But there was something about this contact that made it clear this wasn't another server, even before Noah smelled the too-familiar cologne.

"How've you been, baby?" Roman murmured.

"Leave me alone, Roman. I'm at work." Noah bit back the

please that had risen instinctively in his mouth. It wouldn't have been about courtesy, but about supplication, and he wasn't desperate enough for that, not yet.

"You want to get together when you're *not* at work? We could catch up on old times."

"No. I don't."

Roman sighed, clearly disappointed. "You can't still be mad at me, Noah. You're a smart guy; you know none of that mess was my fault. I didn't force you to do anything, did I?"

"No, you didn't." It was a hard truth, but not one Noah would let himself ignore.

"So what are you mad about? Why can't we be friends?"

"I'm not mad about then, I'm mad about now. I've told you to leave me alone, and you won't, so that's what I'm mad about."

"But why do you want me to leave you alone in the first place, if you're not mad about the stuff before?" Roman had a way of talking that made it seem like he was working with a stupid child. Annoying, but also strangely flattering, because at least he cared enough about you to try to fight through your ignorance. At least, that was how Noah had felt when he'd been younger, getting to know Roman for the first time. Now? Now he just wished the damn bartender would hurry up with the drinks.

I want you to leave me alone because I don't like you, Noah thought, but he just said "I'm at work. I need to concentrate on my work."

"Oh," Roman said. "Work. Right." He leaned in a little closer, his body completely lined up against Noah's now. "I'll come back after your shift, okay? We'll hang out."

"No," Noah said. "I don't want to hang out with you." And then, before he could catch it, he said, "Sorry."

"Don't be sorry. I know you don't really mean it. I'll see you in a couple hours."

"I'm meeting my boyfriend after my shift. I doubt he'll want extra company." Noah wasn't quite sure where the lie came from, but it shut Roman up, at least long enough for the bartender to get his slow ass in gear and hand the tray of drinks to Noah.

"Boyfriend, huh?" Roman said as Noah turned away from him. "I'd like to meet him."

"I only introduce him to friends," Noah said, and swept away toward his table.

It was a small victory, and fairly empty, considering it was based on a lie. But even a small, empty victory was better than none at all, and Noah went about the rest of his shift with a much lighter heart. Roman and his friends left when their dinner was finished, Noah made some decent tips, and everything was fine, right up until he was standing at the bus stop after his shift and an unfamiliar SUV pulled up and rolled down the passenger side window.

Maybe someone looking for directions or something. Noah bent down cautiously and saw Roman smiling at him from the driver's seat. "Get in, Noah. I'll give you a ride."

"No, thanks." Noah stepped back. He knew—*knew*—what was coming next.

And sure enough, Roman put the SUV in park and climbed out, walking around the hood to stand in the misty rain and shake his head at Noah. "I'll drive you to your 'boyfriend'. You don't have to introduce us if you don't want, but I'll get you there all warm and dry. That's nice of me, right?"

"Thanks, but I'd rather take the bus."

"Because there is no boyfriend." It wasn't an accusation, just a statement of fact. "You think I haven't kept an eye on you, Noah? Come on. We're from the same neighborhood, we know the same people. I'd have heard if you were seeing someone."

"I don't think people actually tell you all that much. Just coming from the same neighborhood doesn't mean we're running in the same circles."

Roman shook his head. "No. I know you, and I know when you're lying. You aren't very good at it."

Noah had no real response, and luckily the bus arrived, honking angrily when it found the SUV parked in its pull-off spot, and Roman reluctantly climbed back behind the wheel and pulled away. Noah was shaking a little as he climbed the steps to the bright, safe interior of the bus, but he tried to ignore it. Just like he'd been trying to ignore Roman.

He was so deep in his thoughts that he almost forgot about getting off the bus early, but as soon as he remembered, his brain started singing him a newer, better song. *Got to avoid Roman* was replaced by *Going to see Shane*, and Noah's whole body felt like dancing.

It was a tiny, harmless crush, that was all. He was just having a bit of fun for a change, not throwing his life away. He jumped down the last steps off the bus and jogged a few paces before making himself slow down. He could play it at least a *little* cool, surely.

He was almost to the clinic when he realized there was a strange traffic sound beside him. A car driving too slowly, engine almost idling. He turned his head and saw the SUV, Roman behind the wheel.

He'd never been afraid of Roman. He'd worried about what Roman might do, how he might be embarrassing or cruel or do things to make life more difficult. But he'd never thought Roman might actually be dangerous. Not until this moment.

Noah sped up, but didn't run. He wouldn't panic, wouldn't give the son of a bitch that much satisfaction.

He reached the clinic and banged on the door, a bit too hard, too loud. He heard the SUV door open, sensed Roman coming closer. Damn it, damn it. He banged on the door again, then turned. "Roman, are you serious?" He tried to sound like this was just an unpleasant, pathetic surprise. "You're stalking me, now? I guess I should be flattered, but really I'm more annoyed."

"I just wanted to meet your boyfriend. Remember? You said you were going to see him, but instead you're—at your vet's office? Noah, are you dating a dog? Have things gotten that bad for you?"

And finally, the door opened. Noah kept his gaze on Roman and that meant he got to see the bastard's eyes widen and his smirk fade as he stared over Noah's shoulder.

"You okay, Noah?" Shane asked. He was a warm, solid presence at Noah's back, and it was hard to resist the temptation to lean into him at least a little.

"Who the fuck are you?" Roman demanded. He always got aggressive when he was unsure of things. Noah knew Roman far too well. And, he realized, didn't know Shane nearly well enough. How would he respond to a situation like this?

Fairly calmly, it turned out. "Who am I?" Shane echoed. He sounded amused. "I'm the guy whose doorstep you're standing on. You can tell me what you're doing here or you can fuck off, but those are your only two options." It was all said in a conversational tone.

Roman's attention shifted to back to Noah. "*This* is your boyfriend?"

"He gave you two options," Noah said. His body was shaking, but it didn't come through in his voice. "Talking to me wasn't one of them."

"You think I give a shit what options he gave me?"

Shane moved, then. Of course he did. Smooth and easy, flowing around Noah until he was right in front of Roman, tall and strong, his shoulders so wide Noah would have had to duck around him in order to see Roman. But he didn't duck. He stayed still, and let Shane do—whatever Shane was doing.

"Time to go," Shane said. His voice had the same inflection Roman used so often, making it sound like he was talking to someone too stupid to understand longer sentences or more complicated words. "You're done here."

"Are you serious?" Roman blustered, but Noah could see his feet shuffling backward.

"Unless Noah says otherwise. And I don't think he's going to."

"So you *are* dating a dog," Roman said, stepping back out of Shane's reach and leaning around him, trying to see Noah. "An attack dog. Jesus, Noah, I never knew you liked it rough; I could have—"

"You couldn't have done a damn thing I haven't already done ten times better," Shane said. His voice was a low growl, and Noah wasn't sure whether it was the tone or the words that sent a not-entirely unpleasant chill down his spine. "Noah's through with you, and I don't like you sniffing around. So I'm going to take away the 'tell me who you are' option. That means the only one left is 'fuck off'. So, go ahead. Fuck off."

"Are you fucking kidding me?"

Shane was quiet for a moment, then said, "Noah, maybe you should go on inside."

Noah didn't have time to figure out his own response before Roman spluttered, "What? I'm here to talk to Noah, not you."

"Yeah, but he doesn't want to talk to you, and I'm getting bored with it, too. But it won't look good for Noah's vet school applications if he's mixed up in a beating. So he should go inside."

This time Roman's feet moved back faster and farther. "A beating? Seriously? My dad's a cop, asshole!" Roman was still backing away as he talked. "You want to beat up a cop's kid?"

"Hell, yeah," Shane said. "I was just going to do it to get rid of you, but if you're a cop's kid? That would make it a fucking pleasure."

"Jesus Christ, Noah, you're really scraping the bottom of the barrel, huh?" Another few steps backward and Roman was all the way to the sidewalk. "You're spreading your cheeks for a fucking Neanderthal, now? I mean, you were never more than a pity-fuck, sure, but I didn't know you were *this* desperate."

Shane was a solid wall, not reacting to the insults at all. He just stood and watched as Roman circled around the front of the SUV and opened the driver's door, then stood on the running board and yelled over the hood. "You're a fucking asshole, buddy! You know that?"

"Yeah, I know," Shane said calmly. He raised his hand in a simple wave. "See you around."

There was a moment of hesitation as Roman clearly searched for a way to do more damage without getting his ass kicked; he apparently didn't find one, because he lowered himself into the driver's seat, slammed the door, and revved the engine. He gave them the finger as he pulled away, which was actually kind of funny. After everything else, Roman thought an insulting hand gesture was going to have an effect?

"I'm so sorry," Noah said as soon as the SUV was out in traffic. "I didn't know he'd followed me, or I wouldn't have come here. I didn't want to drag you into this; it wasn't a plan or anything. I mean, all that 'boyfriend' stuff, and then the things he said about you, that was kind of my fault, because—"

"Because you have magic powers that control someone else's mouth?" Shane asked with a raised eyebrow. Then he shook his head. "Don't worry about it. It was his fault, not yours, and it wasn't a big deal anyway. Unless you think he's going to stick around and give you trouble on the way home?"

Shane was worrying about *Noah*. Noah had brought that problem here, dragged Shane into it, and the issue was whether Noah had a safe way to get home?

"I'll be fine," he said. "And you should know, he's a big talker about his dad, but his dad wrote him off years ago. He won't cause you any trouble. And I don't think Roman's really dangerous, just annoying."

Shane looked skeptical. "You know him better than I do. But he seemed kind of—" He stopped, shrugged, and said, "I don't know. You know better, obviously." He didn't sound petulant, just realistic.

"You think he might come after you?" Noah asked. It probably wasn't out of the question. Maybe not Roman himself, but Roman plus a couple of his followers. Which made Noah realize—"He was alone tonight. Roman's never alone."

Shane just stood there, waiting for Noah to say more. But Noah wasn't quite sure what conclusions he should be drawing. "Shit, it's cold out here. Can we go in?"

"Oh, sorry." Shane was still farther from the door than Noah, but he nodded his invitation and Noah headed inside. It was good to be somewhere warm, familiar, and well-lit. He shrugged off his jacket and hung it on the coat rack, scuffed his shoes over the mats by the door, then turned, and was pretty sure his eyes actually bugged out of his head like he was a cartoon character.

Shane was taking his hoodie off. It was a different one than he'd been wearing before, faded blue instead of dingy grey, so probably Shane had gone to pick up his stuff from somewhere while Noah had been at work, but that wasn't what really caught Noah's attention. The fabric was up over Shane's head, so he couldn't see Noah as he stared at the space between Shane's rucked-up T-shirt and the waistband of his jeans. Three or four inches of golden skin and glorious, hard abs, lean and warm-looking and begging to be touched.

Noah swallowed hard and tried to control his expression as Shane pulled the hoodie loose and bunched it in one hand. Damn it. Noah had known Shane was broad-shouldered, obviously, but he guessed he'd assumed that bulkiness continued most of the way down, under the baggy fabric of his clothes. But with just a threadbare T-shirt covering him, it was clear that Shane's broad shoulders and chest tapered fast to a hard, tight waist. Shane was muscular without being beefy, he was tall, he was lean... god, he was perfect.

"You okay?" Shane asked.

It was probably cowardly to pretend Noah's discombobulation had anything to do with Roman, but Noah wasn't brave enough to admit the real cause. "Yes. Thank you." He frowned. "I mean, really, thank you. That was great, and I'm sorry he was so rude to you."

"Rude?" Shane grinned, a sudden flash of beauty that was only partly due to his white teeth. "I've been cursed out worse than that by people I call friends. That was no big deal."

"I'm sorry if he—if I—I mean, I'm gay. I'm not hiding that. But it must have been a bit weird for you when he assumed you were, too. A lot of guys wouldn't take that so well."

Shane frowned, looking uncertain for the first time that evening. "Not such a weird assumption," he said, then nodded toward the back of the clinic. "Dodger's asleep on my bed, and the other animals seem okay, but do you mind having a look at them?"

Right. That was why Noah was there. "Yeah, sure," he managed. And he tried to keep his mind at least somewhat on the job as he followed Shane back through the clinic. *Not such a weird assumption*, he thought. The words echoed and twisted in his mind, bouncing back to him in shimmering rainbow colors. *Not such a weird assumption. Not such a weird assumption.* It wasn't anything conclusive, he reminded himself. And even if Shane were gay, that wouldn't mean he would ever be interested in a geek like Noah, someone who couldn't even deal with an annoying ex on his own.

Still. *Not such a weird assumption.* It wasn't definite, but it was definitely intriguing.

Feral

Chapter Seven

THE ANIMALS IN THE cages all seemed fine, according to Noah. That had been what Shane had thought, really, but it wasn't like he knew a damn thing about anything. So even though Noah was careful to say that he wasn't an expert himself, it was still good to hear his opinion.

"And Dodger's sleeping," Shane said, nodding his head toward his room. "Is it okay if you look at him, too? I mean, he's supposed to still be tired, right? But he used to wake up whenever I woke up; he *woke* me up a lot of the time. But he's fast asleep, now."

"I can look at him," Noah said. "But Dr. Anderson checked him before she left, right? She would have caught it if there were any problems. And when the tech comes in, you should check with her, too."

Shane nodded. "Yeah," he said. "Okay. And you've got to catch your bus, right?" It wasn't like Noah was Shane's slave or something. "Thanks for coming by, though. I appreciate it."

"So—" Noah tilted his head a little, kind of like Dodger did when he couldn't figure out what Shane was up to. "Do you not want me to look at him, then?"

"What? No, I do. But only if you have time."

"God, Shane, of course I do. I mean, I'd be happy to see him even if you *hadn't* just totally helped me out with Roman, but as it is? I owe you, for sure."

"Nah. You said you didn't think he was dangerous. I probably made things worse." But Shane edged down the hallway toward Dodger anyway, and Noah was kind enough to follow him.

"You didn't make things worse," Noah said as they reached the doorway and peered inside.

Dodger was curled up in the sheets, but he lifted his head and thumped his tail against the air mattress when he saw his visitors. He didn't get up, though. Didn't come running across the room, his whole body curving and wagging and happy the way he used to.

So Noah and Shane went to him, both crouching beside the mattress as if they were saying their prayers or something.

"Even if things *are* worse, I wouldn't care. It was still worth it," Noah said.

It took Shane a moment to figure out what the hell Noah was talking about. "With the guy, you mean? Roman? That's his name?"

"Yeah." Noah reached out and ran a hand over Dodger's body and the pup rolled over onto his back, inviting a belly rub.

Then Noah used his thumb to lift the dog's lip up, exposing his gums. "Nice and pink," he said. "That's a sign that the blood's in the tissues where it should be, not leaking out because he's bleeding. He seems okay to me, really. And it's not surprising that he's still a bit tired, right? This time last night he was hooked up to an IV, fighting for his life."

Just last night. So much had happened so fast, it was hard to believe it had been just yesterday they'd come to the clinic and Dodger's treatment had begun. "When you put it that way, it seems better," Shane admitted. He twisted around so he was sitting on the mattress and laid his hand on Dodger's warm puppy belly. "Thanks."

"Thank *you*," Noah replied. It seemed like he was going to stand up, then, but instead he shifted around the same way Shane had and rested his butt on the mattress. He didn't seem totally comfortable, but he didn't stand up, either. "I'm feeling stupider and stupider about the thing with Roman—bringing him here, hiding behind you like I did—but you were great. Seriously. You picked up on what was going on, and you played it perfectly. That was fantastic."

Well, obviously Noah was being generous, but Shane shouldn't let himself believe the exaggerations, no matter how kind, so he changed the subject. "How long's it been since you guys broke up?"

"Uh… about four years."

Shane stared at him. "Four *years*? And he's still acting like that? Are you shitting me?"

Noah looked uncomfortable. "It's a bit of a mess."

"But, four *years*? How old were you? How long did you go out for?" He caught himself. He wasn't usually a big talker, definitely not a big gossiper. "Sorry, this isn't any of my business."

"No, it's okay. I kind of made it your business, didn't I?" Noah sighed and relaxed a bit on the mattress. "We went out for about three months. He was my first real boyfriend, I guess, and I thought—I don't know what I thought. I was pretty head-over-heels, I guess. He seemed really—sophisticated, maybe? I was a hard-working little nerd, only worrying about my marks and, like, whether *Iron Man 3* was going to be consistent with the storylines in *The Avengers*. And then Roman—I don't know, he noticed me. I felt like I'd been invisible my whole life, and suddenly someone could see me."

Shane nodded. He thought about himself when he'd been younger, before he'd started growing and gotten big enough to damn well insist people pay attention to him on the rare occasions he wanted them to. Nobody had been willing to see a scruffy, hungry kid, because if they'd known he existed they'd have to do something about him or else admit they weren't going to. Much easier to be blind and walk on by. Someone who saw you? Yeah, that was a gift. Still, clearly it wasn't a gift that had kept on giving, not in Noah's case. "So things were good for a while, and then went bad?"

"Yeah," Noah said. "They went really, really bad."

Shane's imagination tried to fill in the blanks, but he couldn't get a clear picture. "You said he isn't violent…"

"No. It was—" Noah shook his head and smiled uncomfortably. "I've honestly never talked about this to anyone who didn't already know. Four years later, and I'm still acting like it's some big secret. And I know it's not. It's not a big deal to anyone but me, and my family. Compared to stuff other people have gone through, it's nothing. I know that."

Kind of a polite way of saying that Shane was way more messed up than Noah. Hard to get too offended by an observation that was so clearly true. "You got over it," Shane said. "Whatever it was, you got past it. Doesn't mean it didn't suck at the time, though."

"Yeah," Noah said. He sounded almost surprised, like maybe he'd thought Shane wouldn't understand. "And it wasn't so much that the trouble was that bad—I mean, it was bad enough, for sure, but not *that* bad—but it's just that I felt so stupid. I should have known better. I totally *did* know better, but I ignored my common sense, my morals, everything that should have been important to me, all because I thought I was in love with some guy who turned out to be a total asshole."

"I think teenagers are kind of expected to do stupid shit," Shane said as gently as he could. "I mean, there are levels of stupid, but being stupid about your first boyfriend? I think that's pretty standard territory."

"Were you ever?" Noah asked. His voice was too quick, like he was trying to deflect from his own story, or was somehow nervous about the question he was asking. "Stupid, I mean? About a—a boyfriend, or a girlfriend, or whatever?"

Shane shrugged. "I don't know. Not really in that area, maybe. But mostly because my stupid kind of expands beyond one single department, you know? Like, I'm just stupid across the board, so it's hard to kind of break things down into specific reasons."

"You don't seem stupid to me."

"You haven't know me too long. I've had a good couple days." A good couple days that included breaking into a veterinary clinic in order to hang out with the puppy that got poisoned because of his stupidity of the days before. Yeah, he was on a roll, turning over a whole new leaf. Right. But Noah didn't need to hear any of that crap. "How bad did it get?"

Noah didn't answer right away. He and Shane had been taking turns rubbing Dodger's belly, and Shane pulled his hand away now, letting Noah have the contact if he wanted it. Instead of reaching out with his hand, though, Noah bent over and nestled his face right into the ruff of fur around the dog's neck, took a deep breath of puppy-air, then sat up again. "He stole a car. No. He stole the keys, gave them to me, and *I* stole the car."

Shane raised an eyebrow. "That's a level of stupid I can relate to."

Noah's smile seemed a bit more relaxed than it had before.

"It was a teacher's car. She'd given Roman a bad mark on a history essay, said it was nicely polished but had no real content—which, looking back, seems like a pretty good description of pretty much everything Roman has ever produced—and he was pissed off. So he went in to conference with her after school, and when she left the room to make a photocopy of the essay he stole her keys out of her purse and walked out. I was waiting for him; he tossed me the keys and said we needed to go. He said—" Noah shook his head, clearly amazed and disgusted by his younger self. "He said he *needed* me to drive him. He didn't come right out and say he'd stolen the keys, but I knew. I knew it wasn't his car, or one of his friends', I knew he kept looking over his shoulder toward the school and telling me to hurry up. I knew something was wrong, but I just—I thought it was more important to give him what he needed."

"Was there some reason he couldn't drive himself?"

"Yeah," Noah said ruefully. "If he drove himself, it would just be him who got in trouble. But with me driving, he got to spread the chaos and destruction around, and *that* was what he really needed."

"Sounds like a great guy."

"Yeah, he's a prince." Noah kept his gaze on Dodger, his long, agile fingers gently twisting the pup's fur. "And I was a terrible driver."

"Oh, shit, you crashed?"

"Yeah. I think that was part of his plan, too. Maybe. I mean, it sounds crazy, because he was right there in the car so he was risking his own safety, but that wasn't a thing for him. He's just— he thinks he's bullet-proof, invincible, completely immune to reality." Noah glanced over at Shane, looking for something— reassurance, maybe? Shane nodded in what he hoped was an encouraging way, and Noah's shoulders relaxed a little. "He kept telling me to go faster, to take crazy turns, weave in and out of traffic. We ended up most of the way out in the country, going way too fast, and I lost control of the car. It flipped. I got pretty banged up and I can't remember all the details, but I remember hanging there, upside down, my seatbelt holding me in place, and I remember him *laughing*. I couldn't feel my legs, we were both bleeding and messed up, and Roman thought it was hilarious."

"Sounds like a total psycho," Shane said.

"But not just him, right?" Another quick look before Noah continued. "I mean, I knew, and I went along with him. He told me to go faster, but I could have told him 'no'. Obviously. I mean, it seems obvious now, but at the time? I just—he was Roman. He needed me."

"And driving fast feels pretty good," Shane added.

Noah looked almost startled, then nodded. "Yeah. That's right. It felt good."

"Short term gain, long term pain," Shane said. After a moment of silence he prompted, "What happened after that?"

"Confusion, sirens, flashing lights. Bouncing around in an ambulance, then more pain at the hospital and my mom crying her eyes out. Doctors, lawyers, and the bills that go with them. First offense and the teacher was really kind, so I got a diversion program. Community service, counselling—that sort of thing. But my grades dropped far enough that I didn't get the scholarships we'd been counting on. So kind of a mess all around."

"No criminal record, though? That's good."

Noah's expression was pretty hard to read, but he didn't look exactly pleased.

Shane tried again. "The whole thing is very bad, though. Definitely a mess. Just—not as bad as it could have been. Right?"

"Are you just patronizing me, now?" Noah looked amazed, and maybe—hopefully—amused. "I bare my soul to you and tell you my deep, dark secret, and you think it's not that big of a deal?"

"No!" Shane said quickly. "It's very bad. Very dark. You're a troubled young man, Noah."

"I'll have you know, my mother was *very* upset about this. And my sister, too. It's been really—" Noah stopped, looked down at Dodger, then looked back up. His eyes were wide as he said "—inconvenient." A deep breath, a nod as if confirming a realization. "It has been really, truly *inconvenient* for me and my family."

"You're holding up pretty well," Shane offered.

And then Noah laughed. A bit louder and a bit longer than really made sense, to be honest. He rolled back on the bed and Dodger found enough energy to waddle over to him and lick his face, and that just made Noah laugh more. Shane watched him curiously, and eventually, Noah pulled himself together.

"You have no idea," he said, his voice still almost cracking with amusement. "I mean—shit. You're right. I made a mistake, and I paid for it, and I guess I'm still paying for it, since I'm totally broke all the time. And my mom and my sister are paying for it, too, because my mom's still trying to dig herself out from under the bills. But nobody's dead, right? We're paying for it *financially*, but that's all. It's not a tragedy, not at all. Right?"

"It's really bad," Shane said. Then he shrugged. "You know. Kinda."

"Right," Noah said, and he let his arm flop sideways on the bed. "Wow. That's..." He looked up at Shane. "Four years," he said. "Four years I've been carrying that around with me, beating myself up about it. But it was just a stupid mistake, right? I fell for the wrong guy, did something stupid, and—that's it. That's all."

"Probably not too easy to leave it behind when he's still chasing around after you."

"Or maybe he's chasing around after me because he can tell I haven't left it behind." Noah pushed himself upright, clearly excited by the new idea. "I honestly think that might be it. Roman can smell weakness, and it's like catnip for him. Stressing me out was a fun game. But if I'm not stressed anymore—if I can just not worry about him, or about me, or about how bad he was for me— then there's no more fun, right?"

"I have no idea. Maybe?"

"I think so." Noah flopped back down on the mattress and stared up at the ceiling. "I think that's it. Wow."

Dodger had come back over and was snuggled in against Shane's hip, now, and Shane shifted gently and then lowered himself down so he was lying just like Noah was, his back on the mattress, his legs dangling down to the floor. It felt good to lie there like that, with a puppy and a—a friend? Maybe, yeah. A new friend, a different kind of friend. Someone who needed to be protected in a different way than most of the people Shane hung out with, someone who was still fresh and new and clean.

Shane had helped him, at least a little. The face-off with the asshole ex hadn't been a big deal, but Shane had been there and Noah seemed to think he'd done the right thing. And then talking about stuff—well, that had been all Noah, really, just figuring shit out on his own, but at least Shane had been someone to talk to. So, yeah, he was being a bit helpful. A bit useful. It felt good.

"We're still going out tomorrow morning, right?" he asked. "We're going to find some people, talk to them about their pets or whatever? That's still on?"

"For sure," Noah said. He sounded kinda dreamy, like maybe his enthusiasm had worn him out and he was about to drift off to sleep. Shane was surprised by how much he liked the idea of Noah sleeping in his bed.

"Good," Shane said.

Everything was going to fall apart. It would all go to hell. He needed to remember that and not get too attached to anything. He knew better.

But for just right then? His puppy and his friend, a warm,

dry place to sleep and a plan to do something useful the next day? Just right then, it was perfect. A perfect moment. They didn't come very often, and they didn't last very long, but as long as he remembered that, maybe he could let himself enjoy it at least a little.

Chapter Eight

NOAH WANTED TO STAY in the bed forever. Maybe at some point he'd roll over and find Shane watching him, heat in his eyes, and things would continue from there. Or maybe, since he was dreaming anyway, he'd imagine himself as someone a little braver than he was. Well, a lot braver, really. Maybe imaginary Noah would roll over and Shane *wouldn't* be watching him, but Noah would stretch out his hand, and touch—oh, he'd touch that little sliver of warm skin between Shane's jeans and his T-shirt. And Shane would open his eyes, not surprised, just as if he'd been waiting for Noah to do it. Noah would slide his hand—shit, how direct was imaginary Noah going to be? Slide his hand up, or down?

"Did you miss your bus?" Shane asked. Real Shane. Damn it.

"Oh." Noah rolled until he could fish his phone out of his pocket and see the time. "The first one, yeah. But there's another coming in fifteen minutes."

"Okay. And you're definitely not worried about that guy—Roman—being out there? You don't think he might have waited for you?"

"I really wouldn't care if he did, you know? I mean, I almost hope he did, just so I can, like, not care *right in front of him*. Does that sound crazy?"

"I'm not a good judge of that."

"Why not?" Noah looked over at Shane and for a moment, worried that maybe he'd hit a touchy subject. A lot of street youth struggled with mental illness, didn't they? What if Shane actually *was*—well, not 'crazy'. If Noah was talking about a person, he'd never use that word. But what if—

"I just don't know what your rules are. You and him and people like you. So I don't know if you'd be breaking those rules, or how big a deal it would be." Shane sat up, careful not to disrupt the dozing puppy at his side. "Like, I'm probably being a bad host by your rules, right? I mean, I guess I'm a bad host by any rules. No food or anything, you have to sit on the bed because there's no chairs—"

"I like your bed," Noah said, probably too quickly. He tried to fight back his blush. "I mean, it's comfortable. Room to spread out, or whatever." Was he making things better or worse? "Even if you had a chair, I'd probably want to be—" He stopped. Not *in your bed*, he told himself. Wrong words. Wrong words. "—with the puppy," he managed, and leaned over at the waist to bury his flaming face in Dodger's fur. It was only as his face arrived that he realized just how close the pup was to Shane's body. Was that Shane's hip Noah's head was jammed against? Of course it was.

Jesus. He needed to get himself under control. No more talking would definitely be a good idea. But also, clearly, no more moving around, since he couldn't be trusted to maintain any sort of personal space boundaries. If Dodger had been on Shane's lap, would Noah have just jammed his nose into the poor guy's crotch?

Probably, he reflected, and a tiny part of him wished the damn dog had been just a little more affectionate.

"I should get going," he said after he'd hidden his face for as long as he could justify.

"Okay," Shane agreed. He sounded cautious, which wasn't exactly shocking, considering how Noah was acting.

"Thanks for everything. The animals seem fine. I'll see you tomorrow." As he sat up, Noah's hair brushed against Shane's upper arm and he felt his face heating again. He was such a loser.

"You okay?" Shane asked.

"Yup. Just—gotta go!" Noah scrambled off the mattress and headed for the door. He was aware of Shane following him, a graceful panther following a clumsy, half-panicked baby giraffe. When they reached the front door, Shane caught Noah's arm, and for a moment, everything stopped except for Noah's racing brain. Noah needed to get away, because if he stayed he'd embarrass himself. But Shane was touching him! Shane wanted him to stay!

"I know you said you weren't worried," Shane said gently, "but let me go out and check the street, okay? Just to be sure? Even if you *do* want to run into him, it'd be good to do it with a little warning, right?"

Noah's brain was so scrambled he could barely remember who the hell Shane was talking about. But when he did finally think about Roman, he didn't feel the familiar tightening in his shoulders, the urge to hunch over and make himself smaller, less noticeable.

Maybe his newfound confidence would abandon him as soon as it was tested, but for right then, he felt strong. "If you want," he told Shane.

"Or I could walk you down to the bus stop. Yeah, that's a good idea. This is an okay neighborhood in the daytime, but at night it's a bit rough."

"This feels like one of those puzzles where there are wolves and sheep that have to get across the river," Noah said as lightly as he could. "Because if it's a bad idea for someone to walk alone in this neighborhood, we're kind of screwed."

"I don't follow."

"Because *you'd* be alone," Noah said. "I'd be fine, because you'd be with me, but then I'd get on the bus and you'd be walking back here alone."

"Oh," Shane said. "No, that doesn't count. That's not a problem."

"Why not?"

"No one's going to mess with me. You're all—I don't know, you're all tidy and everything. You look like you'd have something worth taking. But nobody's going to bother with someone who looks like me."

"Really?"

"I'm big enough to not be an easy target, and ragged enough to not be worth taking a risk on. So I'm good. But you're not doing so well with either of those. Give me a second to grab my sweatshirt and I'll walk you."

"It's raining," Noah tried as Shane jogged back toward his bedroom.

"It's Seattle," Shane called back to him. A moment later he'd returned, pausing for a moment to pull his hoodie over his head before adding, "If I didn't go out in the rain, I'd be stuck inside all winter."

"That's not really the message the tourism people want us to be sending," Noah chided as they stepped out into the drizzle and Shane turned to lock the door. Noah flipped his own collar up to protect his neck as Shane pulled his hood up, and then they started down the street.

It felt good to be walking with Shane.

And after saying goodbye at the bus stop, riding home, going to bed, jerking off furiously to the thought of touching Shane, waking up the next morning and jerking off in the shower to the same thoughts, eating some breakfast and thinking about going back to his room for another round before returning to the clinic, and finally managing to distract himself from spank-bank

Shane by thoughts of seeing real Shane, it felt good to get back to the clinic the next morning.

They set off walking together again, this time in weak but real morning sunshine. Dodger had been left behind as per Dr. Anderson's orders, and every now and then Noah saw Shane pressing against the spot in his sweatshirt where the pup usually rode. The tech who came in on Sundays had agreed to take care of Dodger until she left just before dinner, and Shane should be back well before then. But Shane had clearly still been reluctant to leave the pup behind.

"It's great that you have a dog," Noah said after they'd walked a few blocks.

"Great for me," Shane said. "Maybe not so good for Dodger. He should be with a family somewhere, right? Like, people with kids and a yard and all that."

"I don't know. Dogs want a pack, sure, but I don't think they care too much about the rest of it. He gets to spend almost all his time with you, so that's pretty lucky. For him, I mean. For a dog, to spend time with his owner. That's lucky."

"He should be with someone who keeps him from eating poison, and who gets him vaccinated on time."

"But you're that person, now. You know to watch out for poison, you know what to do if he gets some by accident, and as soon as he's strong, he's getting his shots. So you're doing fine."

Shane didn't look convinced. "If I'd taken him to a shelter they'd have found a *good* home for him."

"No." Noah stopped walking, and after a step or two, Shane stopped as well and turned to look at Noah. "Sixty percent of dogs who go to shelters get euthanized," Noah said firmly. "Sixty percent! Now, sure, some of those are sick or injured. And puppies have better adoption rates than adult dogs. But there are still a *lot* of puppies that get euthanized because nobody wants them. And a lot more that sit around in wire cages on concrete floors for weeks or months, waiting for someone to come for them." Noah took a step closer to Shane. "And even the dogs that *do* get adopted? They don't all go to perfect homes. Some of them get neglected or ignored, some end up back in the shelter when they chew on the wrong thing or have too much energy after staying home in their crate all day and then being stuck back in their crates all night."

This felt important, somehow. It was important that Shane knew he'd done the right thing, and was still doing the right thing. "Dodger got lucky," Noah said with quiet intensity. "He's still lucky. Just because you're lucky too doesn't mean it's not good for everyone. You guys are a good pair. A team. Okay?"

Shane shrugged, but Noah took another step, right into his space, and he was only a little bit aware of how close he was to that rugged body. "I mean it, Shane. Sometimes good things are good for everybody. Seriously."

"That's how it works for you, is it?"

"Oh, give me a break, Mr. Cynical-and-Jaded. Sometimes things are *bad* for everyone, sometimes they're good for everyone, most of the time they're just sort of complicated. I'm not being naïve about this. But you and Dodger? That's good-good. And it's just weak-ass self-pity to pretend otherwise."

Shane's eyes narrowed. "Weak-ass self-pity?"

The warnings were clear. The consequences could be devastating. And still, because he was brave, because he was stupid, or because he just somehow *knew* he was okay, Noah pressed on. "Yeah. That's right. Dodger's fine, so if you keep going on about how tough he's got it, after a while it stops being about him and starts being about you."

"You spend *four years* beating yourself up about one little mistake and then you call *me* out on self-pity?"

"It's a classic takes-one-to-know-one scenario," Noah shot back.

Shane's frown was fierce, his gaze sharp, and still somehow Noah managed to hold his gaze. Finally, Shane turned and started walking again. Not too quickly, though. As if he was waiting for Noah to catch up with him, Noah hoped.

They made it to the next intersection and were stopped at the light when Shane said, "You really think Dodger's okay?"

"I think he's a lucky dog," Noah replied. "Absolutely."

"I've never had a pet before. I just want to do it right, give him what he needs, what he deserves."

"Sounds like a great attitude. You'll be fine."

They walked in silence for a little longer, and then Shane said, "You've got a dog at home? Golden retriever or whatever?"

Noah wasn't sure what to make about the breed assumption; he supposed it was the most white-bread animal Shane could think of. "We had a Pekinese, growing up. But he died a couple years ago, and none of us are really ready for another one yet."

"You're going to be a vet with no pets?"

"No. Once I'm a vet, or maybe even before, if I'm stable enough, I want a lot of pets. But I have to be sure I'm in the right place to be responsible for an animal, first."

Five more steps and then Noah said, "That doesn't mean I have to be sure I have a lot of money, Shane. It means I need to have the time to spend with them. So don't go twisting this around into another round of I'm-a-bad-dog-owner."

Shane made a huffing sound that Noah hoped was a laugh, and they kept walking. Seattle didn't have a really rough part of town, not compared to other cities Noah had visited, but it certainly had parts where poverty was more of an issue, and clearly they were entering one of those neighborhoods.

"There's a couple squats down here," Shane said, "And a park where people hang out. Lena said not to bother with shelters or other official places, because she's already contacted the people who work in them, and because the people there are already getting help. I'm not sure that makes sense, but she's the boss, so we can at least start with the other places. Okay?"

"I'll follow your lead," Noah promised.

"Yeah?" Shane said. He stopped walking and turned to face Noah, looking him over with a critical eye. "Promise?"

What was about to happen? "I trust you," Noah said.

And Shane reached for him. Hands on his shoulders—no, not his shoulders, his head. His hair. Rough fingers combing through, tousling and disarraying.

Shane stepped back and took a long, thoughtful look before shaking his head. "You used to look like a Mormon out doing his Sunday visits. Now you look like a Mormon who just got fucked in a back alley. I'm not sure which is better."

Noah wanted to respond with something clever, some comment about Shane's fucking technique needing work if all it resulted in was mussed hair, but his mouth was far too dry and he ended up just making a sort of mumbling noise.

Shane didn't seem to notice the lack of response. He reached out and tugged the shirt tail of Noah's button-down loose on one side. "I think the just-got-fucked look is our winner," he said, and he crumpled the front of Noah's shirt in his fist and held it, apparently trying to make some creases.

Say something, say something! Say that you want a really authentic look, and there just happens to be a back alley over there. Say it! Say it! "Oh," Noah managed. "Oh, okay." He felt as though he was swaying, a tall tree in a windstorm, but Shane didn't seem to notice anything strange. Really, Shane's general lack of observational skills was the only thing keeping Noah from dissolving into a blob of embarrassment jelly.

"Don't stare at people," Shane instructed. "If anyone's staring at you, just ignore them. Stay with me, and keep your mouth shut until we know what's going on. This is their home, and we're just visiting. We follow their rules, or if their rules are too weird, we leave."

"Okay," Noah said. "But—their *home*?" He looked at the building they'd stopped in front of. It was an abandoned house, set back off the road, windows boarded up, no signs of life. "Here?"

"What'd you think a squat would look like?"

"I never gave it much thought."

Shane led the way around the side of the yard, then laid one hand on the top of the chain link fence and just sort of levitated himself over it. Noah took a deep breath. If he tried that he'd fall on his face. Less embarrassing to climb, so he jammed the toe of his shoe into one of the links and worked his way upward. It was only four feet or so. He should have been able to jump it, and if he'd had a chance to practice first, he would have given it a try. "I'm fairly fit," he told Shane, who didn't seem to be paying much attention. "I'm just not super-coordinated."

"Okay," Shane agreed easily. "This is fine."

Noah jumped from the top of the fence and damn it, his ankle turned a little as he landed, making him stumble. Under other circumstances it would have been lovely to feel Shane's hand gripping his shoulder, helping him balance, but just then, it was one more embarrassment. "I run," Noah said desperately. "I did cross country in high school. I'm not super-fast, but I have good endurance."

"I really hope that won't be something that comes in handy," Shane said, turning and starting toward the back of the house, "but I guess it's good to know, just in case."

Noah managed to stop himself from making any claims about his prowess on the soccer field when he'd been in elementary school, and followed Shane silently. Now that he was paying attention, he could see signs of habitation about the place—a rough path in the grass, two back windows with the boards pried away to let some light in, and there, on the back steps, a fold-up baby stroller. Shit.

"Does a kid live here?" Noah demanded.

Shane nodded. "Yeah. Two of them. And their mom, and their mom's boyfriend, and sometimes other people. I know there's a pet rat, and there's a cat that kind of hangs around, but I don't know if anyone's really claiming it. No dogs, last time I was here. People in squats don't usually keep dogs—they're too loud."

"But—kids? Stroller-sized kids?"

"Yeah, they're pretty loud, too. It's not perfect, but what can you do?"

"I wasn't worried about them being *loud*!" Noah exclaimed. "I mean—why are they living like this? Do they go to school? There are shelters for women with kids, aren't there?"

"Shhh." For maybe the first time since the puppy blood incident, Shane looked genuinely annoyed with Noah. "Keep your voice down, and keep your judgments to yourself. This is their *home.* They're doing their best, and they're dealing with shit in their own way. They don't need you deciding it's not good enough."

Noah felt a flash of hot shame. Shane had given him very simple rules and he'd blown right through them at the first opportunity. "I wasn't judging the *people*," he tried. "I'm just—the system is supposed to be better than this, isn't it? For kids, at least?"

Shane seemed to relax a little. "Things are supposed to be lots of stuff," he said, and he sounded about a thousand years old. "Doesn't always work out too well in the real world, though." He looked toward the house, then stepped back toward Noah and said in a low voice, "Raven's the mom. She grew up in and out of foster care, and she's worried that if she goes to a shelter, they'll take her kids away. I have no idea if that's a real thing to worry about, but that doesn't really matter, you know? She's worried anyway. And her boyfriend, Andy, has a criminal record, and a lot of family shelters are really careful about keeping anyone with a record out. It makes sense, from their side—they're protecting the other people living there. But it's one more thing keeping Raven out. And he can't get a job with a record, so if he's going to find them a better place to live the only way to earn money is to do more crime, and if he gets busted for that then Raven's even more screwed, because she's got to look after the kids so she can't go out and even panhandle or anything." A pause before he added, "I'm not saying any of it's right, but I'm not saying it's wrong, either.

It's just the way things are." He watched as Noah absorbed the new information, the new perspective, then shrugged. "And they've got a rat, and maybe a cat. So—this is a good chance, right? Get the pets to the clinic, let the social workers be nice to Raven and see if she can trust them. If she can? It could be really good for the kids. If she can't?" He shrugged. "At least it'll be good for the rat."

It hadn't seemed real, Noah realized as he trailed slowly after Shane. Back in the coffee shop, talking it over with Lena and Dr. Anderson, it had all just been a theory. The project made sense on paper, and it would look good on his applications to vet schools, so he'd agreed to be part of it.

But here, in the real world? Everything seemed simultaneously more important and more doomed to failure. A mother afraid of losing her children to the system that had brought her up to not trust it. A man who'd committed a crime and was therefore doomed to continue committing crimes, trying to provide for a family that wasn't his.

It was too complicated, too overwhelming. What the hell was safe, studious Noah Reed doing out here, climbing into a squat house through a window because the door had been boarded and nailed shut? Going to visit a woman who was dealing with issues he could never understand, and two children being raised in a life that was a world away from his own, even though their homes were only a few miles apart.

What the hell was he doing?

He was following Shane. That was all he could focus on,

all he could think about. Shane understood all this. Shane was the stationary core at the middle of the whirling maelstrom. This was Shane's world, and as long as Noah trusted Shane, things should be okay.

Feral

Chapter Nine

THERE WAS SOMETHING VERY wrong about the house. Shane had been there before, several times, and he knew better than to expect a tidy, cheerful kitchen with flowers and fresh-baked cookies. But still—there was something wrong.

"Stay close," he hissed to Noah, and then louder, he called, "Raven? Andy?" What were the kids' names? One of them was just a baby, too young to answer, but the other one—"Jayden? You here, buddy? It's Shane. I'm looking for your mom, or Andy."

There was no answer. It wasn't impossible that they were just out. Hell, it wasn't impossible that they'd moved since the last time he'd visited, even though that had only been a few days before. But the house didn't feel empty, somehow.

It was partly the smell that was wrong. The house was a wreck, full of mould and rot and other dank, musty smells, but there was something sharper, this time. Something that made the hair on the back of Shane's neck stand up.

He thought about sending Noah outside, but of course Noah

would want an explanation, and Shane wasn't ready to say that Noah should leave because the house smelled wrong. So the two of them moved cautiously through the kitchen and into the central hallway.

The family was in what used to be the living room. Raven, and both kids, all huddled on the same mattress, and for one gut-sinking moment Shane thought they were all dead. But then the littlest body stirred, wailed a desperate, weak note, and flailed its arms a little.

"Raven, shit," Shane said as he fell to his knees. He scooped up the baby as gingerly as he could, feeling a heavy, over-used diaper leaking something out on his arm and realizing he couldn't worry about that right then. "Raven?" He stretched a hand out and found her skin clammy, but not as cold as he'd feared. "Jayden?" The boy stirred just a little when Shane touched him.

"I need the address," Noah said desperately, and Shane turned to see him on his cell phone. "Shane, where are we? What's the address here?"

For a split second, Shane tried to think of another option. An ambulance meant the hospital, and it probably meant cops poking around the squat, kicking the family out, maybe sending the kids to the foster care Raven feared so much. But there was no way around it. "I don't know the street number. Give them the intersection, and tell them we'll meet them out front."

Noah did that, and a moment later said, "Is it an OD? Shane, they want an idea of what's wrong with them. Is it an OD?"

"Jesus Christ, Jayden's four years old! He didn't fucking OD! I don't know what it is—I don't—" And then he did know. Because little Jayden, lying there, so weak, so pale, dark bruises showing on his skin now that Shane's eyes had adjusted to the dim lighting—Shane had seen that before, too recently. And he thought of the last time he'd seen Raven and the kids. Andy had brought home dinner, fish and chips he said he'd bought but that Shane had figured came from a dumpster, because Andy never had much cash. Shane had eaten some fries, but he couldn't stand fish and had left it alone. But Raven and Jayden had eaten it. And so had Dodger. "Jesus Christ," he whispered, and it felt closer to a prayer than any words he'd said in a decade. "Tell them it might be mouse poison. Rat poison. Tell them it might be whatever Dodger had."

Noah looked stricken, but he relayed the information in a voice much steadier than Shane could have managed.

"And the baby's maybe just hungry," Shane said. "I think he's still just nursing. So, would the poison have gotten to him? I don't know. But it's probably been a while since—"

He stopped talking. The whole thing was too much. The stench of the room, blood and puke and shit and whatever the hell else was coming out of these damaged bodies, the darkness, the thought that this might have been fucking *deliberate*, someone putting poison in food that could be easily scavenged by a human—he stood up, the baby still in his arms, and brushed past Noah. Three steps out of the room, two more down the hallway to the front door. Nailed shut, inside and out. Shane barely slowed down. One hard kick, the weight of his whole body behind his leg, and the door shuddered and began to give. Another kick and daylight streamed in through the cracked doorjamb. The third kick brought the whole thing down in a shattered, tangled mess.

Too late, Shane realized he should have put the baby down before he started kicking, but the little guy seemed fine. The air streaming into the house was fresh and cool, and Shane crouched down long enough to slip the baby out of his filthy, heavy diaper. Shane's hoodie was already disgusting from what had leaked out before but it would have to do, so he pulled it over his head, swaddled the baby as well as he could, and picked him up again. "Jory," he remembered. Raven and Andy, Jayden and Jory. "You're going to be okay, Jory," he said, and he took a step or two back toward the living room, far enough to see Noah crouched beside the bed, holding Raven's unresponsive hand.

The ambulance came, the paramedics quick and efficient as they gathered their patients, but right behind them came the police, and Shane had to fight the urge to run. Maybe Noah realized that, because he stepped closer and said, "They need to talk to you. They need to figure out where the poison came from, if that's what this turns out to be. There could be more out there, or it could happen again if they don't figure it out."

Shane nodded, but he could feel his heart rate speeding up, feel his chest tightening.

"Are you the father?" one of the paramedics asked as she lifted Jory from his arms.

"No. I don't know—there's no father." There was Andy, but he wasn't around. Unless—

"There are bedrooms upstairs," he said to no one in particular. "There might be more people." Andy had eaten the fish, for sure. And there'd been a lot of it. Would they have shared it with anyone else?

He turned and started for the stairs, but he was shamefully relieved when one of the cops stepped in front of him. "We'll check it out," the older man said. He sounded almost nice, but Shane knew how quickly that could be turned off when it wasn't useful anymore. "My partner's going to drive you and your friend to the hospital in case the doctors need to ask you any questions. And if this turns out to be poison, we're going to need to talk to you at the station about that."

Of course they were. And they'd take his name, and find his record, and then they probably wouldn't believe a word he said.

"No problem," Noah said, easing into the conversation. "Anything we can do to help."

Sure, no problem. Everything was fine. Shane tried to take his mind somewhere else as he followed Noah and the other cop down the front walkway to the police car. He tried not to panic as the cop opened the back door of the car and waited for Noah and Shane to slide inside. *No handles, no escape.* At least he wasn't cuffed, he told himself, but the molded plastic seats, easy to hose off, the mesh between him and the driver, the whole goddamn situation—

"You okay?" Noah whispered as the officer shut the door behind them and started around the hood.

"I fucking hate cops," Shane said. It was mostly true. Hate, fear—they were pretty close. "Cop cars, cop stations, cops in general—nothing good ever happens with cops around."

And then the driver's side door opened and the cop took his seat. "You guys ready?"

Shane wondered what would happen if he said no. If he flipped right out, demanded to be let out of the car, would he get his way? He wasn't under arrest for anything, so the cop couldn't hold him, right? But when had cops ever followed the rules when they weren't convenient?

"We're fine," Noah said. "Thanks."

Shane didn't bother to contradict him, but he also didn't relax as they drove to the hospital. Special parking right near the door, because of course cops didn't have to park out with the commoners, and then weird looks from everyone as the cop herded Shane and Noah into the building.

Damn it, hospitals made Shane almost as edgy as the police did. Dealing with both together was a special treat. More moulded plastic chairs in the waiting room, and then the cop got a call on his cell and stepped away to take it. Shane's legs were tense, his brain commanding them to stay still while every other instinct was screaming at them to run.

"We're okay," Noah said quietly. "We haven't done anything wrong, and we're helping them out. Be cool, Shane."

"You think any of that actually matters to them? We haven't done anything wrong? They can always find something, or make it up." Shit, shit, shit. This was not good.

"You have to talk to the doctors," Noah said calmly.

"You called Dr. Anderson. She's coming, right? She knows more about this than I do—they can just talk to her!"

"Then you have to talk to the police. Come on, Shane, you know this. If there was poisoned food somewhere, the police need to track it down. Other people could be sick, and they need to look into that. They need to hear what you know."

"I don't know anything," Shane tried, but if even Noah didn't look convinced, there was no way the cops would believe him.

They sat there until the officer came back from his phone call with another man, a bit older and heavier, wearing a suit but with a holstered gun on his hip. Shit. This was big enough to rate a detective. Shane had never really dealt with anyone above beat cops before this, and he'd really been hoping to keep it that way.

The detective stood in front of Shane, looking down at him. It was hard to fight the urge to either stand up or shrink away, but Shane kept his body perfectly still, only tilting his head to look up at the armed man.

"The other man—the boyfriend," the uniformed cop said. "Andy. Do you have a last name for him?"

Shane shook his head. "No, I don't think so. Just 'Andy'."

"Can you give us a description?"

"Yeah, sure. He'll be the guy puking up blood and shitting it out all over the place. That's Andy."

"Hair color?" the detective prompted, clearly not too impressed with Shane's responses so far.

Shane sighed and gave up. "Blondish, I guess. Light brown, maybe?"

"Height?"

"Shorter than me, but not really small. Maybe 5'10"?" He nodded in Noah's direction. "About his height."

"Build?"

"Kinda—I don't know, kinda round?" Andy was an expert food scavenger, and generally kept the best of what he found for himself, if "best" was interpreted to mean "highest calorie". "He eats a lot of junk food, when he can. Pretty bad zits, across his forehead especially."

"Age?"

"I don't know—twenty, maybe? About my age."

The detective's expression was impossible to read. "Are you aware of any family in the area? Is he from Seattle, originally?"

"I have no idea. I never heard him talk about family, but we weren't super-close friends. He might have some."

"But you can't help us find them."

"Why do you need his *family*? I mean, why do you need a description at all? Seriously, just look for anyone who's coughing up blood. If they look like they've got fucking Ebola, bring them in! Is that so hard?"

"We think we may already have found him," the detective said carefully, and Shane knew. It had been creeping up on him through the conversation, an awareness he'd tried to push away and ignore. Now, he just sat there, numb, as the cop said, "A John Doe matching that description was brought in a few hours ago. Deceased, the body found on the street not too far from where the family was living. We're looking for some help identifying the body."

It wasn't like it was the first time someone Shane knew had died. It wasn't like he and Andy were all that close. But it was just so senseless, so absolutely unnecessary. "From eating the fish?" he asked, his voice a whisper. "From poison?"

The detective shrugged uncomfortably. "I don't think they've got a cause of death yet. They were worried about contagion for a while, and that slowed everything down. But he looks a lot like these victims. The bruising, and the rest of it."

Shane nodded, and waited for the numbness to spread. It was a useful protection tool, he'd always found. Better to feel nothing than to feel something as ugly as this. Finally, he said, "You want me to ID the body? Is that what you're getting at?"

"Just a photograph. Someone's bringing it over now. We can find a private room, if you want to be somewhere less public when you look at it."

No. He didn't want to make it a bigger deal, not when his

defenses were doing such a good job of cutting him off from the event. *Just some guy*, he reminded himself. *Everyone dies sometime.* "I can look at it here," he said. *No big thing.*

The detective nodded and wandered off to find the photo or do whatever else cops did when they weren't harassing people, and Shane let his eyes close. He'd known things were going too well. He'd known he shouldn't get comfortable, shouldn't start thinking the world was a happy place. Assuming Dodger got completely better, the poisoning had worked out pretty damn well for Shane: he hadn't gotten sick, and he'd found a place to live and a part-time job because of it. But Noah had been wrong, with all his talk about things sometimes being good for everyone, with no downside. This had been good for Shane, but bad for Andy. Bad for Raven, and Jared, and bad for little Jory, who hadn't even eaten any of the damn food. God, was that the price required for a storage room and a crappy temporary job? Someone should have told Shane about it, and he absolutely wouldn't have made the deal.

"I'm sorry," Noah said, and Shane was almost startled to realize he wasn't alone.

"Not your fault," he muttered.

"I'm not sorry like an apology, I'm just really sorry this happened to your friend."

"He wasn't that close of a friend. It's not a big deal."

Noah didn't say anything to that, which was definitely a relief. He wasn't a bad guy, at all, but he was kind of clueless, and

Shane was in no mood to listen to one of his crazy speeches about good in the world.

So they sat there quietly together, and after a while the cop came back and showed Shane a photo of Andy, all pale, with bruises around his closed eyes like he'd been beat up. "Yeah, that's him," Shane said, and they left him alone for a while. Dr. Anderson arrived, gave Noah a hug and rested a hand on Shane's shoulder like she thought he needed comforting, or deserved it, and then she went and talked to the doctors.

After a while another uniformed cop came by and said the detective wanted to talk to Shane and Noah at the station, and by that point the numbness was truly doing its job, so Shane just calmly agreed and followed the guy down to the car and went for a little ride. Noah came with him, but of course the cops separated them at the station, taking Shane into one of their rooms with the mirrored wall and asking him a bunch of questions. It was friendlier this time than any other times Shane had talked to police, and when the detective from the hospital figured out he hadn't had lunch they came up with a sandwich and a can of Coke for him. And the first few questions were easy: when had he last seen the family, what had they eaten, why had Dodger eaten the fish when Shane hadn't? But then things got trickier. Where had the fish come from? It felt weird to call a dead guy a liar, but Shane really didn't think Andy had bought it anywhere. Andy never had that kind of money. He'd scavenged it, but it had seemed clean, well-put together—not the sort of thing restaurants usually threw out.

Feral

Still, some of the higher-end places were really picky about their food and would throw out stuff that seemed perfectly good. But did fancy restaurants serve fish and chips? Shane had no idea. Maybe it had been a take-out order that got cancelled, or something. Plain white plastic bag, plain white Styrofoam containers inside it. But what did that mean? Where had Andy been before he brought the fish home? What part of town? He had no car and transit cost money, so probably he hadn't been too far from the house, but it wasn't like Shane actually knew that for sure. He didn't know a damn thing that would do any good for anyone.

Still, he answered the questions as well as he could. When it was over and the detective asked how to get hold of him, it was strange to have an actual address to share. But then he realized it might not be completely legal, him living in a place that was zoned as a business or whatever, so he gave the clinic's phone number and address as a place that might know how to get hold of him, nothing more. Besides, he needed to remember that living at the clinic was temporary; no point in acting like he had a right to be there or anything.

When the detective was finally done with him and he made it out of the room, he found Noah waiting for him. "You okay?" Noah asked.

"Yeah, I'm fine. It's not like I'm a suspect or anything— they didn't rough me up."

"No, I meant—you know. About Andy. And Raven and Jared. I talked to Dr. Anderson, and she said Jory was just dehydrated and hungry; he didn't have any of the poison in his system. And Raven and Jared are responding well to treatment. We found them in time, she thinks."

It was good news, of course, but not as satisfying as it should have been. "So what happened with Andy? If Raven and Jared are okay, why not Andy?"

Noah sighed. "Maybe he ate more of the fish, or maybe he just metabolized it a bit differently. Just bad luck, I guess. Or good luck for Raven and Jared, if you want to look at it that way."

Shane didn't want to look at it any way; he just wanted to forget all about it. "You ready to get out of here? They said you could go?"

"Yeah, a while ago. I was just waiting for you."

It was kind of nice, having someone waiting for him. But in this situation, probably not the best thing. "I've got to go see some people," Shane said. "Check on them. You know."

"In case they might be sick, too?" Noah looked genuinely concerned. "You really think that's a risk?"

"I have no idea. Probably not? I mean, I hope not. But I just want to."

"For peace of mind," Noah said. "Sure, that makes sense. Look, if you want, I can borrow my mom's car and drive us around. For something like this, she'd be glad to let me use it."

"No," Shane said. A borrowed car would be just one more thing to worry about, but more importantly, "You don't need to come along on this one. I'm not doing work for the clinic, just checking on some friends."

"Oh. Right." Noah looked almost hurt for a moment, but then he said, "What if someone *is* sick? You don't have a phone, so how will you call for help?"

"They're not really going to be sick," Shane tried. "I'm just—I don't know. I just won't be able to stop thinking about it until I check on them, so I'm going to check on them. For me, not them."

Noah nodded, and for a moment, Shane thought the conversation was over. But then Noah said, "Yeah. So, not for you, but for me, because I'm not going to be able to stop thinking about it if I don't know you're okay, can I come with you? I mean, if you absolutely don't want me along, or if you think your friends would really not like me showing up, then, okay, I guess I just have to deal with it. But if you're mostly neutral and you think it wouldn't be that big of a deal for your friends, can I come?"

It made no sense. Noah was worried about Shane? The other way around, sure, but what the hell? "What do you think is going to happen to me, exactly?"

"We already established that, right? It's not about what's going to happen to you, it's about how I'm going to be wasting my time worrying about you."

"Okay, but I'm worried that my friends might be poisoned. You're worried that...?"

"Monsters might get you? Aliens? Or, I don't know, maybe

the person who put the poison out? I mean, if this actually was deliberate, someone trying to poison people instead of mice, then there's a psycho out there."

"And what exactly are you going to do if we run into him?"

Noah held up his cell phone like it was a cross to ward off vampires. "I'll call the cops, then scream for help while you fight him. It's an excellent plan."

It was a ridiculous plan, but somehow, Shane didn't want to point that out. He thought of walking Noah to the bus stop the night before, something that wasn't strictly necessary but had made him feel better. He'd always been a bit protective of others, always the one to put himself between his friends and trouble, and it was strange to have someone trying to protect him. Strange, but not exactly unpleasant.

"When you scream, will it be really shriek-y and hysterical? Because that's what I'm looking for in a bodyguard. If the screaming isn't shriek-y, you don't care enough about your job."

"*So* shriek-y. You won't even believe it, seriously." Noah's eyes were bright, and Shane liked being the person who'd made them that way. They widened with artificial innocence when Noah added, "Do you want a sample? I could throw something together for you right here, if you want."

"I'll trust you," Shane said. It felt good to have someone walking beside him. And that was enough of a reason to ignore his better sense.

Feral

Chapter Ten

COMPARED TO THE SQUAT house, the low-rise apartment building Shane took Noah to seemed pretty nice, at least until they opened the broken security door and stepped into the front hallway. It had been the odor that had seemed to tip Shane off to something wrong at the house, but here, he didn't seem alarmed by the stench. It was a strange mix of cigarette smoke, stale urine, and either cumin or body odor. Noah's nose tried to curl away from it, but Shane headed for the stairs without apparent concern.

"This is Tristan's apartment," Shane said as they climbed, "but there are usually lots of people here. It's like a commune or something, except Tristan is the only one who really pays for anything. Cold nights there'll be, like, ten or fifteen people camped out on his floor. Sometimes people try to take advantage and I have to toss them out, but mostly everyone knows the rules."

"He has a job? That's how he pays the rent?"

Shane was in front of Noah, but even without seeing his

face Noah could tell Shane wasn't sure how to answer. They stopped outside a doorway on the third floor and Shane shrugged as if he'd decided to tell the truth and knew Noah wasn't going to take it well.

Noah schooled his face to neutral, mild interest and Shane said, "He's a whore. Like, a pro, not someone who just takes some cash now and then." Apparently Noah was doing a good enough job of seeming un-shocked, because Shane continued. "He's got some good clients and could probably afford to live somewhere nicer, but then his neighbors would complain about all the lowlifes he lets into the building, so he stays here. That's the kind of guy he is, you know?"

Noah wasn't really sure he did know, but he nodded anyway. "And you're the one in charge of making sure nobody's taking advantage of him?" he asked.

Another shrug. "Not, like, officially. I'm not his pimp or anything. But he's too nice for his own good, and other people are assholes sometimes. So—yeah. I help out."

Noah knew his jealousy was unwarranted and petty, but that didn't do anything to help control the emotion. Shane protected Tristan. Hell, Shane protected Dodger, and this whole mission was about protecting his friends, and he'd gotten himself a job protecting the clinic. Shane was protective. Of everyone. Shane had stepped in to help Noah out the night before because Shane was Shane, not because Noah was Noah.

Noah was still trying to control the negativity when Shane raised his hand and knocked twice on the door. Then he paused and knocked twice more.

"Is that a code?" Noah asked.

"Sort of, I guess? It's just how we all knock. He used to leave the door unlocked, but strangers kept wandering in and sometimes they were hard to get rid of."

The door opened, then, a too-thin girl with rainbow hair and a lot of blurry eye makeup staring out at them as if she'd just woken up. Or maybe as if she were stoned.

"Hey, Becks," Shane said easily, and she nodded a vague sort of greeting and stepped aside to let them in.

Noah followed Shane into an inner hallway, narrow and poorly lit, with a line of coat hooks strung along the entire length of one wall. There were about six jackets hung up, a couple of them still dripping water onto the linoleum floor.

The hall opened into a living room where one long couch stretched along the far wall, with a collection of arm chairs scattered around elsewhere. There was a little kitchen at the end of the space, and a stub of a hall that clearly led to a bathroom and bedroom. And there were half a dozen people in the living room, all watching as Noah looked around his new surroundings. The apartment itself was just dingy and underfurnished, but the people? Noah didn't think he was cool enough to even know the right word to describe the sense of style they all seemed to share. Lots of piercings, lots of tattoos, lots of skimpy black clothing and lots of brightly colored hair.

"This is Noah," Shane said. "I work with him."

Maybe not the most glowing introduction, but it was enough to bring one guy up out of the arm chair where he'd been lounging. He didn't have the tattoos or piercings that the others had, but still, as he crossed the room with his hand outstretched, it was hard not to stare at him. High cheekbones, blond hair styled in a deliberately mussed imitation of bed-head, and brilliant blue eyes topping a smile that seemed completely genuine and downright angelic. "Hi, Noah," the beautiful creature said. "I'm Tristan. Welcome."

Then the guy turned to Shane and reached out a gentle hand to touch his chest. Oh. To feel the space under his hoodie. "Dodger?" Tristan asked, clearly prepared for bad news.

"He's okay," Shane said quickly. "He's good. But—" He stopped for a moment as if hoping to find a way out of telling the rest of his story. Then he shook his head. "Shit. Dodger's okay, but he ate poison. That's what made him sick. And the thing is—" He half-turned so he was facing the whole group. "I need to talk to you guys."

"What's going on, Shane?" Tristan asked. His voice was low, almost intimate, and he stepped a little closer with a concerned frown.

"Shit," Shane said, mostly to himself, and then he shook his head. "Can we sit down? I have to tell everybody what's going on."

So they sat, and Shane spoke. He told his friends about visiting the squat, finding the victims, going to the hospital, talking to the police—all of it. No one seemed to have been all that close to Andy, so there were no tears, but Noah was too focused on Shane to really notice any other reactions. Once Shane got started, he seemed okay, but after a while Noah wondered if he was maybe a bit *too* calm. He seemed numb, detached from it all, and that wasn't right, surely. But who was Noah to give advice to someone else on how to handle something like this?

"It was really poison? For sure?" one of the girls on the couch asked, and Shane nodded.

"I guess they're not sure if it was on purpose, but, yeah, definitely poison. They probably got sick about the same time Dodger did, but they didn't have anyone to get them to the doctor. I should have—"

"Stop it," Tristan said at the exact same time Noah said, "No." They looked at each other, then turned their attention back to Shane.

"You couldn't have known," Tristan said gently.

"Sure I could have. I knew Dodger was sick, I knew he'd eaten the same food they had. Fuck, the vet even told me he'd probably eaten the poison a few days ago. If I'd fucking thought about it for half a second, I could have at least gone to check on them."

"Dogs get into rodenticides all the time," Noah said. "We told you it was probably something he picked up when he was walking around, didn't we? So you were just trusting what we told you. That's not your fault."

"It's my fault for listening to you instead of thinking it through myself," Shane said. He sounded exhausted, and Noah wanted to hug him, or offer some other comfort. But he wasn't sure the gesture would be welcome. And, really, he kind of wanted to turn the hug into a bit of a shake; he'd only known Shane for a couple days, and already he was getting frustrated with the guy's attitude. It *was* a form of self-centeredness, thinking every problem in the world was his fault.

"You saved Raven and the kids," Tristan said. "That's pretty important."

"Just by accident," Shane replied. "It's not like I went over there because I thought they might be in trouble. I was just—" He stopped talking and turned to Noah. "Shit. I went to see if they wanted to take their rat to the vet. Did you see him anywhere? He wasn't usually in a cage, he just ran around and they grabbed him if he was getting into something he shouldn't have been."

"Did they feed him any fish?" Tristan asked.

Shane jumped to his feet. Clearly the rat had eaten the fish, and clearly Shane was ready to go rescue him.

Noah held up a hand and pulled out his cell; he resisted the temptation to point out that he *was* turning out to be useful. "I have Detective Brennan's card. I can call him and ask if they found a rat. Going over to the house probably won't work—wouldn't it be a crime scene or something? Or at least there'd be police officers there, looking for evidence, maybe?'

Mentioning the police presence had the desired effect on Shane, and he calmed down at least a little. But he still paced around restlessly while Noah made his call.

"The family had a pet rat," he told the officer after identifying himself. "He probably ate some of the fish, too. We're just wondering if he's been found. I guess he probably would have been loose in the house."

"White rat?" Brennan said. "The guys thought he was probably a pet. I'm sorry, son; we found the body, but he was dead. Lab guys said rats can't vomit, so poison affects them even worse than other animals."

"Okay, thanks," Noah said. He almost wished he hadn't called; it would have been easier if Shane could have heard the news from someone else, not him.

"Hang on," Brennan said before Noah could hang up. "Look, son, the more we find out about this, the more it seems like the poison was deliberately aimed at humans, not animals. I can't get into all the evidence with you, but we're calling this a murder investigation. We need to figure out where the victim found the food. The lab's doing what it can to narrow things down, but most cases are still solved by finding the right people to talk to, not by CSI tricks."

"Okay," Noah said cautiously. "So what does that mean?

Like, why are you telling me about it?"

"Well, in this case, I think the right people to talk to are going to be friends of Andy's. And the only friend we know of so far is Shane Black, who seems less than happy about talking to us. And I doubt we're going to have much more luck with any other street kids. But I'm hoping maybe you can help us with that."

Such a strange symmetry. Dr. Anderson and Lena wanted Shane to spread information, the police wanted him to gather it. And in both cases, Noah was expected to be the handler, the one who kept Shane on track. Did no one remember that Noah had known Shane for only a couple days? Did they really think he had that kind of influence?

"I'll see what I can do," Noah said. He looked at Shane, who was still watching him anxiously, and remembered he had to break the news about the rat's death. Damn it. This whole situation was getting out of control. Was it possible for him to just walk away, go back to his safe life where the worst he had to worry about was an annoying ex and some financial challenges?

Yes, he realized, it was totally possible. He didn't need to be part of this. He was just a visitor, a temporary part-timer, just like he was at the restaurant. Carrie and Sergei were lifers there, and Shane? He was stuck in this life, here. But Noah didn't really *have* to do any of it.

And knowing that he had a choice made it that much clearer what choice he should make. "I'll try to help," he said into the phone before ending the call. He'd try to help the police, but more importantly, he'd try to help Shane. Not that he had any reason to believe Shane would actually let him.

*****

The rat was dead. Shane couldn't even remember the damn thing's name, and he'd never really liked it, never liked its scaly tail or the way it ran around underfoot and made people worry they were going to step on it. But, still. It shouldn't have died.

"They need to figure out where Andy got the food," Noah was explaining. To Shane, and to everyone else. "If they can discover that, they've got a good chance of finding out who did this, and they can punish him. And stop him before anyone else gets hurt."

"I didn't know Andy all that well," Tristan mused. It was good that he was at least trying; he was a leader, and if he made an effort, other people would as well. "He's only been around for a few months, right? And he mostly hung out with Raven and the kids. Can Raven talk? Doesn't she know where he was?"

"I guess not," Noah said. "I mean, I don't know for sure, but I guess if she already told the police, they wouldn't be asking me, right?"

"And why *are* they asking you?" Trey's tone was more aggressive than it needed to be, as usual, but it was still a good question. And Shane knew Noah needed to have a good answer for it. Trey wasn't as tall as Shane but he was stocky, tough and strong and always too damned ready to prove it. He and Shane had never done more than a little chest-bumping in the past, but if Trey decided Noah was a narc, things were going to get ugly. And Shane had brought Noah here, which meant it would be his job to make sure Noah got out in one piece. Damn, it would feel really good to be able to actually do something, something he knew he was good at, instead of just sitting around and trying to use his brain. A fight would be perfect.

But Tristan would get pissy if Shane started something without good reason, so he just sat there, waiting for anything more aggressive than words, while Noah said, "I think they're just asking *everyone*. I'm not special or anything, I just happened to be the person who called him."

"Yeah," Trey said. "You called him, because you just *happened* to have his card in your fucking pocket. That was pretty handy, huh?"

Noah looked baffled. Shane said, "The cop gave him the card when we were at the hospital today. I saw him. Chill out, Trey." There, that was his duty to Tristan taken care of. He'd tried to calm things down. But now he stood up, his body loose and ready, the adrenaline just starting to flow and glow. "Is there going to be a problem with that?" He kept his stare tight on Trey. *Please* let there be a problem.

"I should chill out?" Trey echoed. He held Shane's gaze for longer than he should have, and Shane tried to keep himself from grinning, showing his teeth and making the dare that much clearer.

Then Trey looked away, stood up and walked over to the window. Damn it. He was backing down. No fight, no fun, just more of the goddamn talking it through.

Still, there was a problem to be solved, so Shane kept a hopeful half-eye on Trey while he tried to get the conversation back on track. "Nobody saw Andy on Wednesday night? Nobody knows where he might have been? And nobody's seen any too-good-to-be-true food left in dumpsters lately?"

There was general head-shaking, and Shane looked over at Noah. Was there more they should be asking?

"And nobody knows *anyone* else Andy might hang out with?" Noah tried. "No ideas, even?"

"He sold for Moby, sometimes," Trey said, and swivelled his head to stare at Noah. "You going to write that down, rent-a-cop?"

"Give it a rest," Tristan said before Shane could jump in, and then he turned his attention back to Shane. "I've seen him with some of Moby's guys sometimes, for sure. So, yeah, maybe that'd be worth looking into."

Shane wasn't sure how it had become his job to investigate any of this. But if someone else got hurt because he'd done nothing? Shit. He wouldn't be able to live with himself. "Okay," he said. "I'll check with Moby. And the rest of you—get the word out, okay? Tell everyone to be extra careful about what they're eating, and make sure people are checking on each other—this poison isn't that big of a deal, if you can get to the doctor in time. It just got bad for Andy and Raven because they were all sick at the same time, and they didn't get help."

Another round of nods, then Shane looked over at Noah and pushed himself to his feet. "We good to go?"

Tristan trailed behind them as they headed for the hall, Shane shaking his arms to get rid of a bit of the unused adrenaline. What a waste.

When they reached the apartment door, they all paused, and then Tristan tugged Shane toward him and slipped an arm around his neck. His kiss on Shane's cheek was warm and didn't last long. "It's not your fault," he said softly. Then he pulled away and smiled at Noah. "Get your phone out and I'll give you my number. Shane's a bit stubborn and sometimes he doesn't look after himself like he should. If you see that happening, give me a call and the two of us will gang up on him, okay? He won't know what hit him."

Shane was pretty sure he should object. He and Noah weren't—well, it wasn't completely clear what they were, and it wasn't completely clear what Tristan was *implying* they were, if he was implying anything. But it definitely wasn't Noah's job to help look after Shane. Who, of course, didn't need any looking after anyway. So he should have said something, but he didn't. He just stood there as they exchanged numbers and nods of agreement to some plan he didn't seem to really be part of.

Then he and Noah headed down the stairs and outside. Shane saw Noah take a deeper-than-usual breath of fresh air and felt a sudden wave of self-consciousness. Tristan kept his apartment fairly clean, usually, but the building itself? The building stank. It was disgusting, not the sort of place someone like Noah should be hanging out. That Roman guy was an asshole, obviously, but he had a nice car, nice clothes, and probably a nice family. There were other guys like that, non-asshole versions, for Noah to be spending time with. That was what Shane needed to remember. Noah was hanging out with him because they worked together and because Noah was a responsible, caring person who wanted to help Shane deal with the current situation. That was all, no matter what Tristan had assumed.

"You have to work tonight, right?" Shane asked, and Noah looked startled before peering down at his watch.

"Damn. I'm almost late. I've got clothes at the restaurant, so I can change there, but yeah, sorry, I've got to go."

"That's fine. Thanks for coming by today. And this morning—sorry about this morning. You shouldn't have had to see all that."

Noah squinted at him. "*Nobody* should have had to see all that."

"If somebody hadn't seen it, they wouldn't have gotten help," Shane corrected. "But it didn't have to be you."

Noah looked a bit frustrated, but then he just shook his head as if clearing thoughts and said, "If I walk over to 14th I should be able to catch a number thirty-six bus, right?"

"Uh, I think so, yeah. But I don't take the bus much, so I'm not sure." He didn't take the bus because he had nowhere to go, unlike Noah.

"When should we go out again? I've got school tomorrow and I'm working the dinner shift, but I could come by for a few hours in the afternoon, maybe? And we could go somewhere to talk to people?"

It felt strange to be thinking about the clinic again, as if they were just forgetting about Andy and Raven and the kids. But it was probably all tied together somehow, really. If Raven had known about the clinic, she might have brought the rat in when it got sick, and she and Andy could have gotten treatment as well. Or if there'd been time for the social workers to sneak up on her and get her to trust them, maybe she could have gotten in touch with one of them when she started feeling bad, or maybe there would have been—something. There should have been *something*, and maybe getting the clinic running was as good a way as any to start building a better system.

So Shane said, "Yeah, okay. I'll meet you at the clinic. What time?"

"Two? I won't have much time for studying, but maybe I can do that after work. Or—I don't know. Sometime."

"Okay. Two."

Then Noah headed off to his job, and Shane went to find Moby.

Who, once Shane finally tracked him down in his favorite booth at a local strip club, wasn't too interested in cooperating with Shane's little investigation.

"He's *dead*?" Moby demanded. "Shit. He was supposed to be working for me this week." His expression changed from irritated to suspicious. "You're not just making this up, are you, trying to slide into his job?"

"No. I don't even want the job." Not because it wouldn't be nice to have some cash, but because it would be exactly Shane's luck to get busted just when things were starting to look up. A couple weeks ago, an arrest for selling drugs at some bar or party would have meant free room and board in jail, and nothing more. But now? Shane had a puppy to look after, a place to sleep, and an honest job. He wasn't going to let that get messed up any sooner than it had to be. "Was he working for you on Wednesday? Wednesday night? I'm trying to figure out what part of town he would have been in that night. I saw him around nine/ at his place, and he had the poisoned food on him then. Any ideas?"

Moby had been temporarily distracted by a dancer, but now he looked back at Shane with a sneer. "What are you, then, Sherlock Holmes?"

"I'm just trying to make sure people are safe. Come on, man, your customers could be eating this shit. Pretty hard to deal to a corpse, you know."

"And you're going to be the big hero who saves them?"

"You want to do it? Because, seriously, that would be great.

I've got other shit I'd like to be doing, so if you could take care of this, I'd really appreciate it."

Moby's eyes narrowed and he stared at Shane for a moment before saying, "This is bigger than your usual bullshit. Usually you only get worked up about one person, right? One of your friends, one of the ones you think you're going to save? But now you're moving on to the whole fucking neighborhood?"

"What the fuck does it matter to you? Is there some big secret? Andy was working for you but you don't want to tell me where? Is that it? I swear, man, I don't give a shit about your business or about Andy's. I'm just trying to get this tidied up before someone else gets hurt."

Moby still didn't look completely convinced, but finally he shrugged and said, "He's been at The Skyview Lounge lately. You know the place? I don't know what the hell he was doing at home at nine o'clock at night, though. He should have been working."

Shane thought about it. The Skyview was a dump frequented by junkies and street whores, so, yeah, he knew the place. It was only eight or nine blocks from Raven's squat, and it wasn't like Andy had a perfect work ethic. Going home for a mid-shift break was something Shane could definitely see Andy doing. And if that's what it had been, that meant that the fish had probably come from somewhere between the bar and the house.

Or maybe it had even been *from* the bar. Did The Skyview do takeout? Did they do delivery?

Shane pulled his attention back to the present enough to

thank Moby and head out of the bar, but his mind was forming theories even before he reached the street.

It could totally make sense. It would be too direct for the poisoner to actually work in the kitchen where the food was made—too close of a connection. But what if someone had ordered fish and chips from The Skyview, they got it delivered, the asshole took the food away to check it or whatever, sprinkled the poison on the fish or did whatever he did to it, then took it back out to the delivery guy and said it was the wrong order and he wasn't going to pay for it? The delivery guy would take the food back to the lounge and it wouldn't be worth anything. Someone might have given it to Andy, or sold it really cheap. Hell, maybe they'd traded for a hit of their favorite drug. Andy had taken it home, and everything had gone to hell from there.

It wasn't a terrible theory, maybe. As random psychos went, it seemed a bit safer than going into a store and putting razor blades in Halloween candy or whatever. It was a possibility, at least.

Shane checked his watch. Almost six, and the vet tech had said she'd be leaving the clinic at five. So Dodger was on his own, and Shane didn't like thinking about that. Well, it wasn't like there were going to be other dogs at The Skyview to infect anyone; Shane could go get the little guy and bring him along. Hadn't Sherlock Holmes had a dog? A hound, or something?

Shane wasn't too sure about that part, but his version of detective work was definitely going to be canine-assisted. So he headed for the clinic. He'd get the dog, he'd go to The Skyline, he'd find some clues, and he'd figure everything out. He'd deal with the bad guy and the city would be safe again.

He knew he was dreaming, but it was fun. Fun to pretend to be someone like Noah, someone who actually had plans and made shit happen. So, for a little while, Shane would pretend. And if his make-believe helped get a psycho poisoner off the streets? He could live with that.

Chapter Eleven

"THIS IS COMPLETELY DRIED out," the man said. He pushed his plate away as if the food on it disgusted him. "Is it honestly that hard to cook a damn meatloaf?"

Noah couldn't see a single thing wrong with the man's meal, but he put on his best apologetic face anyway. "Would you like me to bring you something else?"

"I'd like you to bring me a fucking meatloaf special that isn't hard as a chunk of goddamn cement!"

The dirty looks from the next table were sent in Noah's direction, of course. If one of Noah's customers started swearing loudly at a table next to a young family, that was absolutely Noah's fault. "I'm sorry, sir, but could you please keep your voice down? There are children—"

"You're feeding this shit to kids and you think a few strong words are what they should be worrying about? You're trying to fucking poison me and you think I shouldn't be—"

"You haven't been *poisoned*." Noah's voice was too loud,

too strong, and felt completely right all the same. This asshole talking about poison, after what Noah had seen that morning? Hell, no. "If the meal isn't to your liking, I can bring you something else. I apologize in advance for the delay. But please keep your voice down and stop swearing."

The man looked a bit startled, and Noah knew he'd gone too far. This was a customer, and as such, he was always right. Even when he was being a complete asshole. Noah needed to back down, apologize, and figure out some way to make things right.

That's what he needed to do. But what he did instead was stand stock still and stare the man down.

He tried to remember Shane's posture the night before— only the night before—when he'd gotten between Noah and Roman. Shane hadn't been tense. His shoulders had been relaxed, his hands open, not in fists. There'd been no overt threat, just a quiet, confident dominance.

Noah wasn't in Shane's league, he knew. But going up against this guy? Some middle-aged middle-manager eating dinner alone on a Sunday night in a strip mall restaurant? This guy, Noah could handle.

At least he hoped he could. He was damn well going to try.

He hadn't been able to see Shane's expression the night before, but as he made his body relax, he found that his face followed suit. There was nothing to fight about here, there was just reality, and the reality was that Noah wasn't going to back down.

And it worked. It actually worked. The man slumped back

into his chair and Noah felt almost guilty for handing another defeat to someone who'd probably already suffered through too many of them. But then the man looked up at him, sullen and almost pouting, and the sympathy was gone. He was a grown man acting like an angry baby, and it wasn't Noah's fault if that didn't end up working for the guy. "I don't think there's any point in bringing you another plate of meatloaf; it'll be just the same as this. So would you like to eat this, or should I bring you something else?"

The man practically snarled at his plate, but he pulled it back toward him. "Bring me a beer to help wash it down," he ordered. "Whatever's on tap. Something cheap, to match the rest of the damn meal."

Yup, Noah could put up with that attempt to save face, just like Shane had put up with Roman flashing them the finger as he drove away. Being a gracious winner was actually a lot of fun. So he smiled as he headed for the bar, and a couple other servers caught his eye and gave him subtle, congratulatory grins, and he felt like a big damn hero. When he got to the bar he gave the order and then picked up the tray with steady hands. No shaking, no adrenaline. He was calm and in control.

And twenty minutes later, when Roman showed up, Noah wanted to do a celebratory dance. It was a perfect night. He'd gotten to stand up to a customer, and now he got to stand up to Roman. He thought briefly about calling up his second grade teacher, the one who'd told him he should have been held back a year just because he'd written his math answers too messily and she'd thought they were incorrect. Yeah, maybe it was time he gave Mrs. Boate a piece of his mind, too!

He couldn't keep the grin off his face as he delivered entrees to a family of four and used his peripheral vision to see Roman and his entourage finding seats. They were in Noah's section, and he practically skipped with eagerness as he headed over to them.

"Welcome!" he said enthusiastically. "Can I get you anything to drink?"

"You're in a good fucking mood," Roman groused.

Noah beamed at him. "You're right, I am. I see you all picked up menus on the way in—that's fantastic. Do you need a minute before you make your drink orders?"

"Is this because your goon of a boyfriend got in my face last night? You think that proved a fucking thing?"

"He's not actually my boyfriend," Noah said. That's right, he didn't even need the lie to get him through this; that's how strong he was. "He's just a friend. But seriously, Roman, if I'm making up fake boyfriends as a way to get you to leave me alone, it's a pretty clear sign that I'm not even a little bit interested in you, right? So there's really no excuse for you to keep on bugging me."

Roman's blink of surprise felt real, but the hurt expression he adopted almost immediately didn't. "Seriously, Noah, you hate me that much?"

"You can make it all about me, okay? I'm crazy, I'm mean,

I'm focused on my future, not my past—whatever. You don't have to make this some insult to your ego. It's not you, it's me. All that stuff. The thing is, though—it's been four damn years since we were going out. *Four years.* Seriously, dude, I'm glad I was memorable, but the obsession is starting to—well, I was going to say it's starting to get a bit pathetic, but, honestly? It's been pathetic for quite a while, hasn't it?" He knew he should stop, but now that he was rolling, he just wanted to pick up speed. "I know a girl who has a sort of therapist-life-coach that she says has really helped her. You want me to get the number for you?"

"When did you get so mouthy? You pick this up from your fucking boyfriend?"

"Not my boyfriend, remember? I mean, I'm not saying I'm not interested—did you see the body on him? But as of now, not my boyfriend. I think the mouthiness is coming from me, mostly. Interesting, isn't it? How sometimes all it takes is one little hole in the dam and then suddenly water's gushing out like a river." He stopped himself. He really *was* gushing a bit too much. "Anyway, drink orders, anyone?" He glanced at the entourage and said, "I should mention that I'll be checking ID for anything alcoholic. And if anything looks fake, I'll have to refuse to serve you until the police come and confirm that the ID is genuine."

"Are you fucking kidding me?" Roman demanded.

Noah tried to control his smile, but he didn't try all that hard. "Oh, that's right. You're not twenty-one until December, right? Wow. I think I've seen people serve you alcohol in here before—you must have a pretty good fake ID. But I expect the police will be able to see through it. Should I give them a call and we'll find out?"

"You're a little bitch, you know that?"

Noah remembered Shane's response from the night before and gave up trying to keep his grin undercover. "I know," he said calmly. "So, do any of you want to test your IDs, or are we going for soft drinks?"

"This is bullshit," Roman growled. "I should talk to your manager."

"Sure, okay. Be sure to mention that we've been serving you on a fake ID for months, now. I think he'll really get a kick out of that."

Roman pushed his chair back with a noisy clatter. "This place has *terrible* customer service," he said loudly.

"Tell me about it," Meatloaf Man responded from across the room.

Noah almost laughed. The worst that could happen was that he'd lose his job. A job he hated and wasn't all that good at, a job that didn't really make him that much money, a job he didn't actually have time for now that he was working with Shane. He almost wished the manager would wander out from his little office in the back and make a scene so Noah could channel all the energy coursing through him and use it for a big "You can't fire me because I quit!" scene.

But the manager didn't come out, and Roman and his

entourage left without too much more fuss, and after a little while, Noah calmed down enough to be glad he still had a job. He'd ask for fewer hours, but he'd still try to work a shift or two a week. He wasn't sure how long the job at the clinic would last, so it was smart to have a backup plan.

And he hadn't had a total personality transplant; he still wanted to do the smart thing. No, he was still Noah, still careful, still looking to the future. But he felt like a better version of himself, someone stronger and braver than he'd been before.

It wasn't right to give all the credit to Shane. Noah barely knew the guy, and, honestly, there had to be something pretty bad going on with him, something that had sent him to the streets instead of letting him grow up safe at home. It wasn't like Shane was Noah's hero.

And it wasn't like Shane was Noah's boyfriend. But it had felt pretty good to hear Roman keep calling him that, even after Noah had set him straight. So, not a hero and not a boyfriend, but—maybe a little something of both. Something that was enough not to actually *give* Noah courage, but enough to activate courage Noah'd already had, buried away somewhere. And if Noah was being brave? He remembered his fantasies, remembered thinking about sliding his hand up over Shane's exposed skin.

No, he wasn't that brave. But maybe he could do—something? Maybe?

Then his mind snapped back to the morning, and Shane's reaction to it all, and he felt ashamed for thinking about his own lust when he should have been worrying about all the people affected by the poisoner, and all the people who might still be affected if the psycho wasn't caught.

Shane had more serious things to worry about than some white-bread nerd perving on him. Noah knew that. He picked up the tray of food from under the heat lamps and headed back out to the dining room, and he smiled to himself. Yeah, Shane had more important things to worry about, and Noah would try to help him with those. But was there really any harm in slipping a little perving in on the side?

*****

The Skyline didn't do takeout, and they didn't do fish and chips. And there wasn't anyone in between The Skyline and the squat that sold fish and chips, either. Shane had worked his way up and down the grid, checking every possible street Andy might have walked down on his way home from The Skyline, and he'd found nothing.

He felt like an idiot. All his Sherlock Holmes bullshit, and he'd been completely wrong about the whole thing. "I have no idea where he found the fish," he told Dodger, but the puppy didn't even wake up. He was inside Shane's hoodie where he damn well belonged, but that was the only thing that was going right about the whole night.

But when Shane made it back to the clinic after his exhaustive trudging up and down all the possible routes between the Skyline and the squat, there was someone familiar waiting on the doorstep, and suddenly the night didn't seem quite so dark anymore.

"I think maybe the poison came from a returned order," Noah said as Shane turned onto the walkway and headed for the front door. "I mean, it's one possibility, right? One way for someone to get access to food without working in the kitchen? We had a guy at work today who almost sent his food back, and there was nothing really wrong with it, so probably one of the kitchen staff would have eaten it if it had gone back, but he could have done anything to it while it was at the table. That's what made me think of it." He stood up and shifted from foot to foot. Cold, probably, but maybe just restless. "I came over to mention that to you. That's all. I mean, you don't have a phone, so I couldn't call. So I got off the bus. I hope that's okay."

"It's fine," Shane said. "Did you have to wait for long? Sorry I wasn't here."

"No, not long." Noah shrugged. "A while, I guess. But it's no big deal. It's not like you're—well, when *are* you supposed to be here, exactly? You're being a sort of security guard, right? Do you have set hours?"

Shane brushed past Noah and unlocked the door. "Nobody's going to break in at this time of night, when there are still people walking around."

"No, I didn't mean you weren't doing your job! I was just—making conversation?"

They were inside, now, and Shane dug around to get a good grip on Dodger and set him on the floor, then pulled his hoodie over his head and hung it on the hook by the door. Noah was a bit slow, just like he'd been the night before, but eventually he kicked himself into gear and took his own jacket off, then crouched down to greet Dodger. "He seems really good," he said, looking up at Shane.

It had been so long since Shane had felt it that he barely recognized the faint stir of desire in his body. Something about Noah, kneeling like he was—okay, it wasn't exactly a difficult code to break, but why was Shane thinking about it now, when he'd been in so many other situations that were way more sexual and had affected him so little?

"Yeah, I think he's better," he said. He'd think about his physical reaction later, or maybe not at all. Probably not at all, really. Temporary glitch, nothing to get excited about. "I mean, he still needs the Vitamin K, Dr. Anderson says. But it's just pills, now. He's doing fine."

"Roman came to work today," Noah said. Kind of a disorienting topic change, but Shane nodded anyway, and Noah added, "I told him off. I mean, I don't think I was totally rude, but—maybe I was. And if I was, I don't care."

"That's good." Hopefully the guy would get the message, but if he didn't? Shane liked fighting because he liked fighting, not because of specific targets. But he had a short list of people he'd actually enjoy beating the crap out of, and he was pretty sure Roman was earning himself a place on it. If the dumb fuck didn't get the message Noah sent, Shane would be happy to reinforce it. "And that was a good idea about the poison, too. Kinda weird, actually, because I was thinking along the same lines. But it doesn't actually help too much, because I couldn't figure out where the food could have been ordered from."

Moving by unspoken agreement, he and Noah were heading down the hall toward Shane's bedroom, and when they got there they both found places on the bed and Dodger climbed up between them and Shane told Noah what he'd done with his evening. Noah was a good listener, nodding and encouraging Shane to go on even when he was telling pretty boring stuff, like all the different streets he'd gone down, looking for somewhere that served fish and chips for take-out in plain white Styrofoam containers.

"The cops have probably already done all that," Shane admitted. "I mean, if they're actually taking this seriously, it'd probably be where they'd start, right?"

"It sounded like they were taking it seriously," Noah said. Yeah, Noah was still a bit naïve about the police and the amount of attention they were going to spend on one more dead street person. Shane should have been annoyed by that, but somehow he wasn't.

Noah continued, "But they wouldn't know about Andy working at The Skyline. That's important information, I think.

Can I call them and let them know?"

Okay, Noah's innocence wasn't quite so cute anymore. "You know what I mean when I say he was 'working', right? Like, he wasn't pouring drinks or whatever. He wasn't working *for* The Skyline, he was working *at* The Skyline."

Noah was quiet for a moment, then said, "Are you telling me he was a prostitute?"

Shane snorted. "No. I don't think Andy would have pulled a lot of tricks, not looking like he did. He was just dealing."

"Dealing drugs," Noah said quietly. He let the information sink in for a moment, then said, "Okay, yes, that makes sense. But the police aren't going to care too much about that, are they? I mean, it's not like they can arrest him for it now."

"No. They can't get him anymore." One of the few comforts of death, really. No more cops. "But if you call them with the information, they'll probably want to know how you know. And it's fine for you to say that I told them, but if they come to me, I'm not going to say shit."

"Because you got the information in confidence and don't want to violate that," Noah said slowly.

Shane frowned. "I guess. But also just because *fuck them*, you know? I mean—I don't care if you give them information that might help people, but there's no way I'm giving them anything else. Because fuck them."

"You think the police are your enemies?" Noah was obviously being really careful to sound neutral, and it reminded

Shane of the school psychologist he'd been sent to, back when he'd been going to school. Shane had really hated that psychologist, but he couldn't quite bring himself to hate Noah.

"They're sure as hell not my friends." Shane lay back on the bed, then rolled over onto his side so he could reach Dodger for belly rubs, and so he could look at Noah. Before Shane was even settled, Noah had lain down too, and there they were, horizontal, facing each other, separated by a few feet and a sleepy puppy and nothing else. Shane felt another stir in his groin, and he recognized it right away this time.

"It's not your world," he said. He was trying to make it clear to himself as much as to Noah. "I get that. I mean, I don't really understand your world, but I know it's different than mine. But in mine?" It was strangely important that this be understood. "Noah, I've had cops beat the shit out of me just because I was in the wrong place and mouthed off a little. The last time I was busted, they planted the drugs on me. I'm not saying there weren't other times when I would have had drugs, but they didn't catch me those times, and when they *did* catch me but I wasn't carrying, they didn't let it slow them down. You know? Cops are good for protecting property. People who *own* shit like cops, because cops make sure they get to *keep* their shit. But for people who don't own shit? Cops are—" It wasn't easy to shrug when you were lying on your side, but Shane managed. "They're not my friends. Not at all."

"Detective Brennan seemed okay, didn't he? I can see why you wouldn't want to trust the police in general, but maybe you could be okay with him, at least?"

"He seemed like a cop," Shane said. He rolled over onto his back; he didn't really want to be looking at Noah right then. "But like I said, I don't care if you call him. I just don't want anything to do with him myself. And I don't know how useful the information is, anyway. Andy was *supposed* to be at The Skyline, but maybe he wasn't. He wasn't a totally reliable guy."

"I can tell that to Brennan as well, and let him decide how important the information is. Okay?"

Shane sighed. It was against his better judgement, but considering how poor his judgment generally was, even his 'better' version still wasn't all that good. So he'd let Noah decide this one. "I talked to a few other people, too, and one of them actually warned me about poisoned food, so it seems like the word is getting out there. One of the shelters had people putting up warning posters."

"It was on the radio, too. I heard it at work."

That was something, then. Shane wasn't the only person trying to protect people. He stretched his arms up and laced his fingers behind his head and tried to make himself relax. It wasn't all him. It wouldn't be all his fault if someone else got sick.

They lay there quietly for a while, just the two of them, just being friends. Strange to think they'd only known each other for a few days.

"How old's your sister?" Shane eventually asked. He felt sleepy, and his words came out slow and heavy, like he was dreaming.

"What? She's fifteen." Noah didn't sound nearly as relaxed as Shane was. "Why do you ask?"

"I don't know. Just trying to picture your life, I guess. You guys live in a house, or an apartment?"

"A house. It's the only place I've ever lived."

Well, that was remarkable enough to wake Shane up a little. "Seriously? Just one place for your whole life?"

"Yeah. Why? How many places have you lived?"

Shane hesitated. He wasn't sure what the right answer was. Not just the factually accurate one, but the one that would fit into Noah's understanding, the one that wouldn't scare Noah away. "Quite a few, I guess."

"And your family? Where are they?"

"I haven't got any, really." Shane sat up, then rolled to his feet. He'd practically led them to this topic, with his questions about Noah's family, but now that it was time for turnabout, he realized it wasn't something he wanted to talk about. He hadn't wanted to talk about it with that psychologist years ago, or with any of the social workers who'd tried to dig inside his brain. And he didn't want to talk about it with Noah. At least not right then. "I'm going to go check on the animals. You want to stay here with Dodger?"

Noah struggled to his feet; Shane resisted the urge to help him. "I'll come with you," he said. "And then I guess I should get home."

There was a moment, just a little pause, that made Shane feel as if Noah was waiting for him to say something. But he had no idea what Noah wanted to hear, so he just nodded, and then led the way down the hall to the room where the animals slept.

Chapter Twelve

NOAH'S MOTHER TRIED TO give him privacy. Most of the people he'd known in high school had gone away to college and were living on their own by now. When they came home for summer break or over the holidays, they complained about losing their freedom and having to go back to living like they were children. And then, sometimes, they looked at Noah and seemed to wince. And they were right, of course, that it was a bit restrictive to still be living with his family. But his mother did try.

So that Monday morning, as he stood over the sink and shovelled cereal into his mouth, she didn't ask him why he'd been late getting home from work the last couple nights. He'd mentioned the new job to her, so maybe she thought he'd been busy with that. But there was something about the *way* she was not asking him questions that suggested she suspected something else. Yeah, she tried to give him privacy, but she couldn't just turn off the mothering instincts she'd honed over the last couple decades.

The weird part was that Noah kind of wanted to tell her.

Maybe it was a gay-kid cliché, but he really did get along well with his mom, and she'd always supported him, and it would be nice to share his excitement with someone who'd be happy for him.

But there was nothing to really share, he told himself. He had a little crush. Big deal. And it was hard to tell her about Shane without mentioning Andy and Raven and the kids, or Tristan the benevolent prostitute, or any of the other people he was encountering. Noah hadn't realized how sheltered and naïve he was until Shane held the curtain back and let him see what life was like on the other side of things. And Noah wasn't really sure how to explain any of that to the woman who'd worked so hard her entire life to keep him safe from the very world he was now beginning to explore. He felt as if he was waking from a dream, for better or worse. But maybe his mother didn't need to know about it all, not yet.

"Are you coming home before work?" she asked him.

"No. I'm going to the clinic, to do that outreach thing I told you about."

She nodded. But there were no questions about the program, no prodding about whether he was enjoying it or not. Just a little smile, and maybe a bit of a hopeful twinkle in her eye. She was imagining a simple romance for him, probably; the reality was something much different, but strangely irresistible.

On his way out the door, he gave her a quick hug and a kiss on the top of her head. "I might be late again after work," he said.

She turned away before he could see her full smile, but he knew it was there, anyway.

Classes went by in a blur. He knew he needed to pay more attention than he was, but there was nothing completely essential going on right then, so he could afford a day or two of slight distraction. At least, he hoped he could. Better now than during exams, he told himself. His feelings for Shane were like a fever, and he needed to let them run their course, and then he'd focus on recovery. Or something like that.

The clinic was fairly quiet when Noah got there, which wasn't too unusual for a Monday afternoon. Dr. Anderson was in her tiny office doing paperwork, frowning the way she generally did when she had to look at financial records instead of medical charts, but she smiled when Noah appeared and waved him toward her. "You had quite a day yesterday," she said. "I know that was probably a bit more than you were prepared for. It was more than we expected, obviously; we thought you and Shane might be helping people, but not nearly so directly."

"It was intense," he admitted. "If I'd been on my own, I think I'd have totally freaked out."

"That's funny. Shane said you were really calm and in control; you were the one who phoned for the ambulance, right?"

"Because Shane doesn't have a phone," he said, but even as he spoke he wondered if that was the whole truth. Shane was so determined to be independent, so suspicious of any sort of authority. Maybe he wouldn't have called for help. "And I was far from calm."

"You did what needed to be done, though. That's what matters." She leaned back in her chair and said, "But you don't have to keep going, you know. If this is more than you bargained for, I understand, and so will Lena. If you want to go back to just volunteering here, without the side job, that's totally fine. I don't want you to feel pressured into anything."

Another choice Noah was allowed to make for himself. He could quit his restaurant job if he wanted, he could quit this job if he wanted. He could wrap himself up in blankets and tie pillows to his head and be safe and protected from everything unpleasant, if he wanted. But how could he choose the easy way out when Shane and so many others had no choice at all?

"I'm fine. It was a lot yesterday, but I'm okay. And I think Shane and I are a good team."

"I think you are, too. I'm glad that's working out—I was a bit worried about it, to be honest." She smiled, then said, "He's down at the park with Dodger, if you want to go find him. He said you two were going to work a few hours this afternoon—where are you planning to go?"

"I don't know, really. He's the boss. I just—" *trail around after him like a love-sick puppy. Do as I'm told.* "—follow his lead."

"Let me know before you head out, okay? That situation yesterday made me a bit paranoid—if I'm going to send you into dangerous places, I should at least know where you're going."

Dangerous places? The homes of Shane's friends counted as dangerous? Well, maybe they did, compared to what Noah was used to. "I will. And I can call in and let you know if we change our route or anything."

"Sounds good. I'll see about getting a phone for Shane, too, just so he's got a bit of backup."

Noah wanted to stop her. He liked being Shane's phone-provider; it was about the only useful thing he seemed to add to their partnership. But that was selfish, of course. Shane should have a phone for when Noah wasn't around. And then maybe Noah could call him in order to more easily arrange times to *be* around.

Noah made his way out of the clinic and down to the park. It wasn't actually raining, so he took his time and looked around a little on the way. He'd been volunteering at the clinic for almost two years, walking through this neighborhood at least two days a week, but how often did he actually stop and see it? He remembered his first impressions had been that the area was run down, and his visions of a cushy volunteer experience in a ritzy clinic had required immediate adjustment. But there was more to see, now that his eyes were starting to open.

One of the apartments above the corner store had window boxes, and even in November there were little spots of colour sprouting from them—he was pretty sure they were the ornamental kales his mother was so fond of. The door leading into the next building was painted in a jaunty rainbow of colours, and there was a child's cut-and-paste image of a turkey, the kind made by overlapping handprints, taped to the inside of the window, looking out. The building after that housed a thrift store, and Noah stopped a moment to look through the window at the racks of clothing on display, all styles and sizes.

This neighborhood was home for a lot of different people. It seemed obvious, and Noah supposed he'd already been vaguely aware of it, but somehow he'd just glossed over them, over their realities. He'd seen the shabbiness, but not the rest. There were families living here, little kids growing up happy and loved with their art on display and flowers in their window boxes, even though they didn't have fancy houses or big yards to play it.

It shouldn't have surprised him.

He stopped again just outside the little park and watched another cozy scene as Dodger scampered around Shane's crouched form. The pup seemed completely back to health, darting in and out to nip at Shane's waggling fingers before dancing away. He saw Noah after a moment and gave a happy yip, but waited by his master rather than running over to offer greetings. Shane straightened, for once not lifting the puppy as he rose.

"He's looking good," Noah said.

"Seems like," Shane agreed. Still cautious, like he didn't want to jinx anything. "You ready to go? I have to drop him back at the clinic before we head out."

"No rush." Truthfully, Noah would have been pretty happy to stay there in the little park for quite a while, with the undersized dog and his oversized owner. He crouched to greet Dodger, got a few happy wriggles in return, then straightened. Shane was looking right at him, dark eyes beautiful and deep and completely, frustratingly unreadable.

"A few days ago," Noah started, "I said you should know I didn't mind getting dirty, and you said that wasn't the first thing you knew about me. Do you remember that conversation?"

Shane's expression didn't change as he nodded.

"What did you mean by it?" Sure, Noah felt like a desperate loser for asking the question, but he couldn't figure out any other way to get the answer. "I mean—what had you noticed before then?"

Shane took a moment before he answered, apparently trying to judge Noah's sincerity. Then he shrugged. "I saw you with Dodger, and working at the clinic. I mean, my *first* first impression was that you were an uptight sadist—when you were so happy about taking his blood? But after that? You were nice to him, and to the other animals. So, I don't know. I guess I generally like people who are nice to animals."

"So do I," Noah agreed. The answer hadn't included any of the references to 'your stunning good looks' or 'your irresistible smile' that he might have been hoping for, but it was pretty gratifying all the same. "Do you want to know what my first impressions of you were?"

Shane shook his head pretty quickly. "No, not really."

He bent at the waist and scooped Dodger up, then straightened. "You want to get going?"

"My first impressions were wrong," Noah said. If Shane didn't want details, Noah was happy not to give them, but at least that much needed to be said. "The way you look on the outside isn't what you're like on the inside. Not at all."

Shane kept his face turned toward the dog. "Maybe you don't know my insides all that well."

"Dodger does, though. Right?" Noah reached out and ruffled the dog's ears. "And he trusts you. He loves you. He wouldn't do that if you weren't a good guy."

"Shit, Noah, have you ever even *met* a dog? They love their owners, even when their owners are assholes. Dogs aren't smart about love."

Well, that was a pretty good point. "But they're smart about trust. He's not skittish around you; he knows you're not going to hurt him. You're right, he might love you even if you were an asshole, but he wouldn't trust you, not like he does."

Shane snuggled the pup in a little closer. "He might be stupid about trust, too."

"I don't think he is." And possibly it was time to stop hiding behind a puppy. "I don't think I am, either. I know I haven't known you for that long, but you're a good guy, Shane. I'm really pretty sure about that."

Shane's bashful foot-shuffling was absolutely adorable, but Noah managed to not embarrass the poor guy any further by pointing it out. Instead he said, "So, in the name of being good guys, should we get started? Do you have a plan for where to go?"

"Not a plan, exactly. But I've got a couple ideas."

"Close enough," Noah said. He felt good. Buoyant, almost. The day before had been awful, or at least parts of it had. But this was a new day, and he and Shane were together, and they were friends, and if Noah could ever figure out a way to discover if Shane was actually gay, he could—do nothing, probably, but at least enhance his day dreams with a tiny bit more reality. It would be something.

But it wasn't necessary right then. Shane didn't have to be gay to be Noah's friend, and he didn't have to *want* Noah for them to work together. And apparently, just being Shane's friend and working with him was enough to keep Noah happy.

At least for the time being.

*****

It was a good afternoon. Shane and Noah mostly just walked around, talking to people, and it turned out they were a pretty good team. Shane would usually make the first approach, at least partly because he didn't want Noah getting hurt if one of the people they talked to was having a bad day. Shane wasn't exactly an expert on mental illness, but he'd had friends who could be totally different people on days when they'd had their meds and days when they hadn't, and Noah didn't need to put up with any of that. And even people who weren't mentally ill could still be dangerous if they were assholes.

So Shane did a sort of pre-screening, shuffling up to people in as non-threatening a way as he could manage, exchanging a few words to make sure they were at least willing to be civil, and then backing off and letting Noah take over. The people they talked to tended to keep looking to Shane for confirmation of the whole situation, and he could totally understand that. Someone like Noah, smart and clean and ambitious, telling them stories about a place that gave free medical care to animals and might be able to help people out too, if they wanted—it was clearly too good to be true, or at least too good to be believed without a lot of independent confirmation.

So Shane tried to give that, and Noah provided the technical details, and by the time Noah had to leave to get to his other job, they'd talked to at least twenty people, six of whom had their dogs with them during the conversation. That had probably been the best part, Shane figured. The owners got to see Noah with their pets, got to see how gentle and caring he was with them. A few ear-massages and belly-scratches said a lot more about why he should be trusted than any words ever could.

Noah came back to the clinic with Shane to pick up his backpack, and then he left and Shane stood there, looking after him, and wanting him to turn around. It was stupid. Noah had a life; he had places to be, and he couldn't waste all his time hanging around with Shane. Someone like Shane might blow off a shift at a job he didn't like just because he'd rather do something else, but someone like Noah would show up and work hard. One more reason Noah deserved the success he was heading for, and Shane deserved—well, he was already getting better than he deserved, probably, just with a warm place to sleep and a healthy puppy.

Still, he let himself dream a little. Damn, how long had it been since he'd wasted time on something like that? But if Noah turned around, if he said he didn't need that other job because he was working with Shane, now, and there was no point in him going all the way to the restaurant just to quit in person when he could just as well quit over the phone—if Noah said all that, what could he and Shane do together in the time they'd have found?

Whatever Noah wanted, really. He'd said something about needing to study, so maybe he could do that. Shane couldn't help with anything academic, obviously, but maybe he could figure out some other way to contribute. Dr. Anderson had said she didn't mind Noah spending time at the clinic after hours, so maybe Shane and Noah could lie down on the air mattress in Shane's room, and Noah could—he could use Shane's chest as a desk, maybe. Yeah, he could sit cross-legged, his back against the wall, and he could put his books on Shane's chest and read them there, and one of his knees would dig into Shane's hip while the other nestled into his armpit or something. Dodger would probably be there, too, but Shane would make sure he stayed quiet so Noah wouldn't get distracted.

And then if Noah changed position so he didn't need his

Shane-desk anymore, Shane could—he could make Noah a snack. It wasn't like Shane could cook or anything, but he could microwave popcorn or cut up an apple. He could—

His daydream faltered when he looked out at the street and saw an SUV stopped at the curb halfway to the bus stop. It looked a lot like the SUV from the other night. The bulk of the vehicle blocked Shane's view of the sidewalk where Noah should be, and that was enough to make him worry.

"Stay put," he told Dodger, and he made sure the door shut tightly behind him, keeping the dog inside where he'd be safe. Then he headed down the walkway, out onto the sidewalk, and across the street.

And once he could see clearly, he knew he was right to be alarmed. That asshole from the other night, the one who'd caused Noah all the trouble in the past, was back. Roman. That was his name.

"Hey!" Shane yelled. He didn't run; running was an attack, and he didn't want to do that until Noah was clear of it all. But he walked in long strides, covering ground fast. "What's going on?"

Roman had looked startled at the first yell, but he managed to look smug again pretty damn quickly. "I'm just offering Noah a ride. You don't have a problem with me giving your boyfriend a ride, do you?"

Shane looked around Roman to find Noah. "You okay?"

"I'm fine," Noah said, and it really sounded like he meant it. He took advantage of Roman's temporary distraction to grab his backpack away from the guy. "Roman's being a pain in the ass, as usual, but it's not a big deal. I'm not going anywhere with him."

Stupid for Shane to feel disappointed. Stupid that he'd wanted to get in a fight, wanted to slay a damn dragon or something to protect Noah, who was obviously able to take care of himself. "You're sure?" he said, trying not to sound hopeful. *You're sure I shouldn't beat him up for you? Just a little bit, maybe? I'd stop when you told me to, I promise.*

"I'm fine," Noah repeated firmly. "Roman, I don't want a ride; I don't want anything to do with you. Whatever the hell you've been doing since we broke up? You need to stop it. I'm sick of it."

There was a hopeful moment when it seemed like Roman was maybe going to disagree, maybe even going to grab hold of Noah or do something that would justify a real beating, but then he shook his head. "You really should think this through, Noah. I mean, you're a smart guy, usually. So be smart. Think about your life—the life you want. You really think dating a Neanderthal is going to help you achieve your goals? You planning to take him along when you go to tour vet schools? Going to introduce him to the scholarship committees?"

"I already told you he and I aren't really dating," Noah said. "I just made that up. But it's none of your business, anyway. Seriously, Roman, you think I'm done with you because of Shane? I'm done with you because of *you*. You're an asshole, and I really don't like you, and that's all there is to it. So go away."

Shane tried to focus on the positive. Noah was being strong and taking care of himself. That was good. Sure, it stung a bit that Noah had gone out of his way to make it clear he wasn't involved with Shane, but it wasn't like Roman had been wrong; Shane *couldn't* help Noah with any of his goals, and it was stupid to pretend they were anything more than friends. Maybe not even that. They were coworkers, and Shane just needed to remember that.

It would be a lot easier to accept the twist of disappointment if he had something to distract himself with, so he stepped forward, close enough that he was right in Roman's space. "You heard him," he said, low and threatening. He truly wished Roman would be stupid enough to start something, but he knew he wasn't that lucky. "Go away. You're done here. And if you keep bothering him, I'm going to start bothering you. You know what I mean?"

Roman didn't actually look all that sure what Shane meant, which was fair, because Shane wasn't too sure, either. But he'd be able to think of something, if he had to.

Roman took a step away from Shane and spoke to Noah. "Last chance, man. I really, really think it'd be best for you if you came with me, now."

"Fuck off, Roman." Noah's voice was so clipped, the words enunciated so clearly, it didn't really sound like he was swearing. He was just trying to be as clear as possible.

And apparently he finally got the idea across, because after a brief pause, Roman nodded, then turned and headed for the SUV. "Don't forget that I gave you a chance," he called as he went.

"Sorry about that," Noah said before Roman had even pulled away. "I told him you and I aren't dating. He's just saying it to get to me."

Because of course Noah would be insulted at the idea of being linked to Shane. "No worries." He stepped backward, toward the clinic. "Sorry if I made things worse, coming out like that."

"You didn't." Noah looked like maybe he had more to say, and even though he knew he probably didn't want to hear it, Shane would have listened. But the bus came then, and Noah had to go. "I'll come by after work, if that's okay," he said.

"If you want," Shane agreed. He wasn't going to beg.

"Just for a bit," Noah said. "To check on the animals."

"Okay."

And that was all. The bus rolled into traffic, taking Noah away, and Shane turned around and headed back to the clinic. His daydreams had been stupid. Noah didn't need a Shane-desk, and he didn't need snacks while he studied. He didn't need an asshole like Roman either, obviously, but someone like Noah obviously had a lot more than two choices of who to spend time with.

He'd come back to check on the animals, and that would be fine. Nice, even. Shane could enjoy his company without going off on some stupid fantasy about them being study-buddies or whatever.

Nothing to get upset about. No big drama. Shane didn't need any more people in his life, anyway. He wasn't even doing a good job of taking care of the friends he already had.

*****

It was raining again when Noah got off the bus by the clinic. Streetlights reflected off the puddles, and a warm glow came from some of the windows above the darkened stores. Kind of pretty, in a way he'd never noticed before.

There was a man's dark shape on the sidewalk just outside the clinic, and as Noah turned to go up the walkway, he realized there was another dark shape behind him.

His first thought was Roman with one of his friends, and his second thought was that he needed to run. If he could get to the clinic door, Shane would be there, and Shane would protect him.

But then one of the men stepped closer, and Noah saw the uniform. "Noah Reed?" the policeman said, and Noah relaxed, at least a little. Then he saw the clinic door open and tensed back up. Shane and police really didn't seem to be a good mix.

"Yeah, hi," Noah said, trying to sound casual, trying to let Shane know there was no reason to do anything stupid. "What's up?"

"We need to see inside your knapsack, Noah," the officer said. His voice was calm and invited a reasonable response. "That isn't a problem, is it?"

Noah's brain stopped working properly. This was too far out of his realm of experience, too strange, too incomprehensible. They needed to see his backpack? "Why?" he asked.

A gentle smile. "We're conducting an investigation and we'd like to rule you out as a suspect."

"A *suspect*?" The officer's calm act wasn't working, not at all. Noah wasn't sure what was going on, but he knew it was all wrong. It made no sense. "A suspect for *what*? What are you investigating?"

"We can't really go into it without revealing confidential information. But if you don't mind us looking through your backpack, we'll be able to move on to more likely avenues of investigation."

That made sense, didn't it? Sure, it did. They just needed to move on, needed to eliminate Noah as a suspect. "I guess—" Noah started, and then, in about two long strides from the clinic door, Shane was there.

"No," Shane said. His voice wasn't loud, but it was strong. "He doesn't consent. Do you have a search warrant?"

"Go back in the building, please," the officer who hadn't been speaking said. He stepped around Noah, got between him and Shane, and tried to stare Shane down. "This is an official police investigation. Do not interfere. Go back in the building."

"It's okay," Noah said. Everything was happening too fast, and he was suddenly acutely aware of the guns attached to the officers' belts. He'd seen the videos on the internet and knew he had rights he could assert, but it made no sense to do that, not with these men—these *armed* men—standing right in front of him. Best to just go along, surely. "It's okay, Shane. They can look in my bag. I don't mind."

"Film it," Shane demanded. He hadn't moved backward so much as an inch, but he wasn't moving forward, either. Noah hoped that was enough to keep this from turning into something bigger. "With your phone. Or else ask for witnesses. A lawyer." He sounded strangely desperate. "You have a lawyer, right? If you want to show them your bag, do it with a lawyer here."

"Is there a reason you'd need a lawyer, Mr. Reed?" the first officer asked.

No, there wasn't. He'd needed a lawyer the last time, when he'd actually done something wrong, but this time? "No, I don't need one," he said. He just needed to get this whole thing over and done with before Shane completely lost his cool. "Do I just give you the bag, or do you want me to open it for you?"

The officer reached for the knapsack Noah offered. "Am I going to find anything sharp in here? Any weapons, or anything dangerous?"

"Weapons? God, no. Um, anything sharp? I don't think so. Scissors, maybe? There might be scissors in my pencil case."

"Shit, Noah," Shane practically groaned. "It's not too late. Say no. Tell them no."

"It's okay," Noah said, trying to calm him down. "They've just got the wrong guy. It's a misunderstanding or something."

Shane stared at him, and Noah stared back, and as he watched, he saw the emotions playing across Shane's angular face. Frustration and fear as the officer pulled on rubber gloves, patted down the outside of the bag and then zipped open a side pocket Noah never used. Resignation on Shane's face as the officer pulled out an unfamiliar bottle, one that looked like the kind the clinic kept—

Oh, god. If Noah's brain had been rattled before, now it shut down almost completely.

"Ketamine," the officer read off the label on the bottle. He looked up at Noah. "That's a Schedule III narcotic, son."

Ketamine. Ketamine, in Noah's bag. In his bag. Ketamine. Illegal drugs, for someone who wanted to go to veterinary school? Noah's future, his plans, his whole life could be shattered as easily as the glass of the bottle.

"It's not his," Shane said, and the words sounded distant as they worked their way past the rushing in Noah's ears. The other officer had his hands raised, now, ready to grab hold of Shane if he moved the wrong way, but Shane wasn't moving. He was just talking, fast and desperate. "That's not his. He didn't know it was there! He wouldn't have agreed to the search if he'd known it was there, right?"

"It's his backpack, isn't it? And he works at a veterinary clinic that stocks ketamine?" The officer had pulled a plastic bag from his pocket as he was speaking, and he dropped the bottle into it with an anticlimactic plop. "Noah Reed, you're under—"

"It's mine." Shane's voice was strong again, the desperation gone. "I put it in his bag. It's not his, it's mine."

The officer squinted at Shane. "That's not the information we've received."

Noah's brain still wasn't working. He was actually a little dizzy and wondered if he'd be allowed to sit down for just a minute. But Shane was going strong, and said, "Your information is wrong. Think about it. I mean, look at him, and look at me. Which one of us is stealing drugs from a vet clinic?"

The officer sighed as if this was more of a complication than he wanted. "You're confessing, then? When you get to the station you'll give a full statement, explaining how all of this was done?"

"Yeah," Shane said, and the officer nodded, then looked at Noah. "You'd better come along, too. If this is just some game—"

"But he doesn't have to if he doesn't want to," Shane said. "He's not under arrest or anything? Right? You can't arrest both of us, can you?"

"We can arrest anyone we believe is involved," the officer replied.

"He wasn't involved," Shane insisted. "Just me, not him."

The officer who'd been standing in front of Shane suddenly moved, like he was a robot who'd just been activated. "Turn around, hands on the wall," he demanded. "When I frisk you, am I going to find anything sharp?"

Noah felt like he was floating above it all, drifting around above the scene, watching. He saw the officers turn their attention away from the skinny little nerd so they could focus on the dangerous thug. He saw the nerd stumble to the side and stand with his eyes wide, trying to understand what had just happened.

Shane had—he'd hidden drugs in Noah's backpack. No, that made no sense. Except maybe it did? Shane had a history of dealing drugs. At least one of his friends was dealing just a few days ago. Shane had been so insistent that the police not look in Noah's backpack. As if he'd known what they were going to find.

Noah didn't want it to be true, but that wasn't enough. Not wanting something to be true wasn't the same as *knowing* it wasn't true. Noah had made that mistake when he was younger, letting himself go along with Roman's insanity, but he couldn't afford to make the same mistake again. If he could pull anything out of that mess with Roman, it had to be that he'd learned to have more self-control, to not let himself go along with someone just because he was charismatic, or beautiful, or because he *seemed* to be—

"Mr. Reed?" the officer who'd searched his bag was peering at him, and Noah tried to look at the man's face instead of at Shane, being prodded along toward the street with his hands cuffed behind him. "My partner is going to take your friend to the station and get started on that process. I'd like to stay here and ask you some background questions, if I—"

"Noah!" Shane shouted from the street, and Noah whirled toward him. He was going to explain, he was going to say it was all a joke, he was going to *fix* this somehow. But Shane just said,

"Look after Dodger, okay? None if it's his fault."

And then the officer shoved Shane's head down and nudged him into the back of the police car.

Look after Dodger. That was what Shane was worrying about. The dog, not himself. Not Noah.

"I have no idea what's going on," Noah said, mostly to himself. Then he looked at the officer. A policeman, someone who helped people. Someone Noah could trust. "What just happened?" he whispered.

The officer raised an eyebrow. "Looks like you just got lucky. If he hadn't spoken up, you'd be the one riding around in the back of a squad car."

Noah stared at him and tried to figure it all out, but he had no luck, and after a few moments, he turned and let himself sink down so he was sitting on the edge of the clinic's front step. He looked out at the street that he'd thought was pretty just a few minutes earlier. What the *hell* had just happened?

Chapter Thirteen

SHANE KEPT HIS GAME face on, but it wasn't easy. He'd assumed he'd be looking at a charge for possession of ketamine, but he hadn't really thought about what else they'd be accusing him of. Like theft, since they were assuming he'd taken the bottle from the clinic's lockup. The cops had contacted Dr. Anderson to get more information on that, and Shane was working pretty hard to keep himself from imagining her reaction. She'd trusted him, given him a damn key to the place, given him a job, taken care of Dodger— and now this. No, it was definitely best to not think about that.

And there were other things he didn't want to think about, too. Other people who'd be disappointed in him. So he sat in the metal and plastic chair at the police station and flexed his wrists inside the handcuffs the cops had left on him after they'd seen his record. The cold metal bit into his skin, and that was good. A little pain was a good distraction.

He wasn't sure how long he'd been sitting there, cuffed to

195

his chair beside a big wooden desk in a room filled with big wooden desks, before the officer who'd arrested him came and took him to one of the smaller interview rooms. There was a man already there waiting for him, slumped in his chair like he was exhausted, wearing sweat pants and an old T-shirt. It took a moment to recognize him in those clothes instead of his suit.

"Detective Brennan," Shane said as he was guided into his own chair. "Right? I tried to forget about you, obviously, but Noah's been chirping away about how hard you're working, trying to figure out who killed Andy." Shane let his gaze run over the man's casual attire. "Round the clock effort, obviously."

"Don't start, son. I'm here to help you out, but if you piss me off enough, I might just go back to my lazy cop lifestyle."

"You're here to help? Yeah, okay." Like Shane hadn't heard that too many times before. "You want to help, you can uncuff me. How about that?"

Brennan didn't even hesitate. He just raised his hand and beckoned to the officer who'd arrested Shane. "Can you get rid of the cuffs, Scotty?"

Scotty didn't look too impressed, but he did it, and Shane forced himself to leave his arms hanging by his sides rather than lifting his hands to rub his wrists. He wouldn't give the cops the satisfaction of knowing the cuffs had hurt.

"So, what now?" he asked. "I turn in my friends or something, and you and I ride off into the sunset together?"

"Now you tell me where the ketamine came from," Brennan said. "And you tell me the truth, son. That's how I help you."

Yeah, of course it was. Shane turned to look at Scotty. "You probably don't want to go far with those cuffs. I've got an idea they're going to get put back on pretty soon."

"I don't need details," Brennan said calmly. "No names, no locations. Nothing that could get anyone else in trouble. I just need enough information to know that these drugs actually are yours, not Noah's."

"How I got them?" Shane squinted at the cop. "Your boys said I stole them from the clinic. Is that not good enough? You said no details..."

"I've spoken to Dr. Anderson. She's double checked. There's no sign of tampering with the narcotics cabinet, no missing inventory. She looked at the bottle and says it doesn't match her marking system. She checks each narcotic shipment herself, did you know that? Hand writes an inventory control number on each bottle. There's a handwritten number on this bottle, too, but it's not in Dr. Anderson's handwriting and it doesn't match her numbering system. So, no, the drugs didn't come from her clinic, son. So I'd like to know where they *did* come from."

Shane wasn't good at this. He wasn't a strategist, wasn't crafty. If a problem couldn't be solved by toughness, it probably wasn't going to get solved, not by him. So, with no idea what to say, he fell back on his strengths, and sat there, unmoving and unmoved.

Brennan nodded as if he'd gotten exactly the reaction he expected. "Why'd you speak up?" he asked casually. "I assume you planted the bottle in Noah's backpack because you didn't want to be carrying it yourself? Too risky to do that when you had a willing stooge like Noah wandering around. But then why'd you confess? If the whole point of the operation was to protect yourself, why'd you speak up?"

Well, Shane didn't have a good answer to that, so he just stared.

Another nod from Brennan. "You know why I'm here, son?"

"Maybe everyone at home is totally sick of the 'son' bullshit, so you had to come in here to find a fresh audience?"

"I'm a homicide detective, s—Shane." A rueful grin at his near-slip was almost enough to make Shane not hate the guy. Almost. "I don't bust petty dealers, and I don't work narcotics. So what the hell am I doing here?"

"Trying to make more overtime money so you can buy a new fucking shirt?"

Brennan looked down at himself. "I like this shirt." Shane raised his eyebrows, but Brennan ignored him. "So, no. I'm not here for the extra cash. I'm here because your little adventure tonight has touched on something larger the department is looking at, and the detectives in charge of that case want you to help them out, and they seem to think there's a better chance of you talking to me than of you talking to them."

"Because of our warm and caring past relationship."

"That's about what I said. But they said as crappy as my chances are, they're still better than anyone else on the force. That sound about right?"

"I really don't think any of you has a shot in hell."

Brennan leaned back in his chair and said, "And I really don't think that was your ketamine. So you can either prove to me that it was, or you can cooperate with our investigation, or you can sit back and watch as we go back to our original suspect, the one who was actually in possession of the narcotics. So you're free to go, Shane. You want to stick around while we book Noah Reed?"

Shane stared at him. "Noah didn't know the bottle was in his bag." There'd been a moment of doubt about that, back outside the clinic, a moment when Shane had wondered just how much vet school cost and whether maybe Noah had needed a little extra cash. It hadn't mattered; Shane would have taken the fall for Noah even if the whole thing had been Noah's idea. But it hadn't taken much thinking for Shane to know that Noah was completely innocent. Of course he was. Noah was smart, and careful, and responsible. He wasn't stealing drugs from Dr. Anderson, and Shane knew that with everything he had. So when he spoke to Brennan now, he was speaking with utter confidence in the truth of his words, and Brennan seemed to accept that. "It wasn't Noah's K."

"So you don't think Noah put the drugs in the bag. And I don't think *you* put the drugs in the bag. But things are pretty awkward for everyone right now, because *somebody* put the damn drugs in the damn bag. I think it's in your interest *and* my interest to figure out who that person is. And that's all I'm asking you to help me with."

Even a few days earlier, Shane would have kept his mouth shut. He would have known no good could ever come from giving information to cops, and he would have sat there without saying a word until they threw him in a cell or out onto the streets. But things had changed. Shane had changed. He still didn't trust cops, of course, and he'd still put himself through pretty much any misery if it meant the cops were suffering along with him. But he wouldn't do that to Noah.

So he shrugged, trying to make it look like no big deal, and he said, "Roman." Brennan just waited, so Shane added, "I don't know his last name. But he was holding Noah's bag earlier tonight, and he's a total asshole who was making threats about Noah regretting stuff. So he probably planted the shit and made a call to the cops to get Noah in trouble."

Brennan glanced toward the mirrored wall, and Shane wondered what signal he was sending, and to whom. Whatever he was saying, he got no immediate response, and his next question was, "Why would Roman want to get Noah in trouble?"

"Because he's an asshole," Shane said slowly. Had the cop missed that the first time around? "He and Noah used to go out, I guess, but Noah realized Roman was a psycho and dumped him. There's probably a record of all that somewhere in your files if you dig around a bit. So Roman's looking for revenge."

"And you think he got it by trying to frame Noah for drug theft?"

The question was so obvious Shane didn't answer. Besides, his brain was going somewhere else, now. He wasn't a thinker, didn't have any of the well-honed techniques that people with education could use. But every now and then, his underfed brain gave him a gift, and he tried to accept it. Now, he frowned, tried to organize his ideas, and then said, "It wasn't random."

"No, we didn't think it was," Brennan said. He sounded a little confused. "Why would someone randomly frame Noah Reed?"

"Not Noah. *Andy.*" He frowned at the table, trying to see the pieces of the puzzle as if they were set out in front of him. "We've been—well, I have no idea what you've been doing, other than watching TV, but me and Noah, we've been trying to track where Andy would have gone on his way home to find the food. But that was assuming that the food was just left out there for anyone to find. A psycho, or whatever. Random. But what if it wasn't?"

He looked at the cop and saw the man looking back at him,

blue eyes focused and intent. "You think someone deliberately poisoned Andy. Someone—"

"They *brought* him the food," Shane said. "That's why it doesn't match with any of the places Andy would have walked to. He didn't go to the food, the food came to him. Someone wanted to poison *him*."

"Why?"

"I don't know," Shane admitted. "I mean, Andy wasn't a saint or anything, but most of the people I can think of who'd have a problem with him would have just kicked the shit out of him. If they wanted him dead, they'd have shot him or something. Poison is weird, isn't it?"

"It is," Brennan mused. "There's a bit of a link between poison and women perps. You know any women who might have had a grudge against Andy?"

"No," Shane said. It was the right answer, the one he should always give when cops asked him questions, but it was also the truth. He didn't know anyone, male or female, who'd be mad enough at Andy to actually want him dead.

Really, if he was right that the poison had been directed at Andy, the smart thing to do was to back off and let the cops deal with it. If there wasn't a random psycho with a grudge against homeless people, everything was simpler. Nobody else was going to get hurt, so why should Shane do someone else's job? Yeah, that was smart, especially when he had other things to worry about. "So, you knew that name. Roman whatever. You recognized it.

Was it the magic word? Was saying that enough to get me and Noah the hell out of this show?"

"I want a statement," Brennan said. He stood up half-way, just enough to lean over and snag a notepad and pen off the counter by the mirrored wall. "And I want the truth, Shane. Right now, you and Noah are clear of it, but if you give me a false statement, if you so much as exaggerate a single word, I'll find *something* to bust you for." He gave Shane a cold look, then added, "We'll be getting a statement from Noah as well. The two had better match."

Shane thought about resisting. Was he legally required to give a statement, and even if he was, did he give a shit?

But he was tired, and really, the night had gone better than he'd thought it was going to when he'd claimed the drugs; it seemed like he was maybe going to sleep in his own bed, eventually. So he could probably do a little favor for Brennan, especially if the favor was something that might end up getting Roman in trouble.

"I'm not very good at writing," he said. "I can't spell for shit. But I can give it a try. What do you want to know?"

*****

Noah's first instinct had been to run home, bury himself under the covers of his bed, and hide. It had seemed ironic, at first, that it was his experiences with Shane that had given him the strength to take a different path. Seeing things through Shane's eyes had helped Noah stand up to Roman, and the success of that was what was giving him the strength to stand up to Shane.

Well, not stand up to him, exactly. But not hide from him. That was the key. Noah had wanted to know *why*, and he'd decided he had a right to hear it from Shane's own lips.

That had been enough to get him to the police station. But once he was there, sitting in the waiting area, brooding about it all, he'd started to see how poorly the whole story fit together. Detective Brennan hadn't seemed too surprised to find him at the station, and when he'd said "We have a few questions for you," Noah had been ready.

"That wasn't Shane's ketamine," he'd said. "It wasn't mine, either. I've been thinking about it, and I think I know who planted it in my bag."

Brennan hadn't seemed too shocked by the new information. "Okay. Come on in the back and we'll get a statement from you."

So Noah had done as he was told, writing out all the details of his past with Roman, all the harassment since they'd broken up, and finally the mess that afternoon when Roman had taken his bag from him. It took a long time, and his hand was cramped by the end of it, but he felt good. Shane was innocent, of this at least, and Noah wasn't letting Roman hide his guilt.

"It's well past midnight," Brennan said when Noah handed him the sheets of paper. "Shane left a while ago—we offered him a ride but he wouldn't take it. I hope you're not going to be quite so stubborn? I'll get a patrol car to drop you at home, if you want."

"Could they take me somewhere else, instead?"

Brennan nodded, and there was something in his expression that reminded Noah of his mother when she was deliberately not prying but thought she knew his secrets anyway. "Sure. Wherever you want."

So Noah gave the patrol officer the clinic address, and as they cruised through the rainy streets, a sense of calm fell over him. The last few days had been full of new experiences, new fears, and new ideas. He still wasn't sure how he felt about most of it, but there were some things he was certain of.

When the car pulled up in front of the clinic, he wasn't even a little surprised to see Shane sitting on the concrete step, Dodger snuggled in against his thigh. Maybe Shane wasn't actually waiting for Noah, but maybe he was.

Noah thanked the officer and climbed out of the car, then walked slowly up the path. Shane stayed still, but watched him come.

"Why did you do that?" Noah asked when he was near enough to know he'd be heard even if he spoke quietly. "You hate the police. Why would you let yourself be arrested like that?"

Shane's hand toyed with Dodger's ears. "It just made sense. You can't be sure with cops. Once you're in the system, they want to make sure you're convicted. It wasn't a chance I thought we should take."

We. Noah gave himself half a second to savor the word, then said, "But that applies to you, too. If you don't trust the police, then... why you? Why is it better for this to happen to you instead of me?"

Shane looked down at the puppy, then back up. "What, are you fishing for compliments now? Come on, man. You know why."

Noah stared at him for long enough that Shane apparently realized Noah didn't know anything of the sort.

"Because you've got a future. You've got plans. You're going to be a vet, right? But even if they didn't charge you, there'd still be an arrest report or something, and you'd have to explain what it was for, and—stealing drugs from a vet clinic, Noah? Come on. That's the sort of thing that could really get in your way."

"But you have a record already. They would have punished you a lot more severely than they'd have punished me."

"That's okay," Shane said. "I've been in jail before—it's not that bad, really. I mean, I'm glad it looks like I'm not going back, but if I did? That'd be okay. It doesn't matter, Noah, not really."

"It *does* matter!" Noah wanted to scream, wanted to cry, wanted to grab Shane by the shoulders and shake him until he saw the truth as Noah saw it. He settled for dropping to his knees so he and Shane were eye-to-eye. He felt the cold wetness seeping into his knees as he said, "It matters to me." But maybe that wasn't enough. "It matters to Dodger, and to your friends. You matter, Shane. You matter a lot."

"Not like—" Shane started, but Noah reached out without thinking and put his hand over Shane's mouth.

"Exactly like," he said. And he held his hand where it was until he was sure Shane wasn't going to argue with him. "No more of that," he said. "If we're going to be—friends, or whatever. Even if we're just working together, you need to stop thinking like that. I have no idea what's happened to you in the past, Shane, but I know who you are right now, and who you are now is someone important. Someone who deserves to have a future, and who can have a future, if he wants one." And probably he'd already pushed enough, but he decided to push it a little further. "Remember how I said that worrying about Dodger not having a good life was a kind of self-pity? Well, you know what? Saying everything is your fault is a kind of the same. It's being self-centered. And assuming that you're not worth anything? It's bullshit, Shane, and you should know better."

Shane was quiet for long enough that Noah felt like he had to take his hand away, even though he didn't really want to surrender the contact.

They stayed there like that, staring at each other through the drizzle, until finally Shane said, "Are you cold? Should we go inside?"

"Jesus, Shane, are *you* cold? Do you think the cold only affects me, or something?"

Shane frowned at him. Apparently he'd taken as much of Noah's lecturing as he was interested in for one night. "No, actually, I'm fine." He leaned back and rested his elbows on the steps behind him and smiled peacefully. "I could stay out here all night."

Noah was shivering. He hadn't realized it, actually, but now that he was thinking about it, he realized that he was freezing. And Shane was trying to make a damn point?

"Okay, fine," Noah said with very little grace. "You're right, I'm cold, even if you aren't, and I'd like to go inside."

"That's all?"

"What? What else do you want?"

"Maybe you want to say 'thank you for being so considerate'. Something like that? Maybe you want to say you appreciate it that I'm looking out for you and *not* being self-centered? Does that sound like something you want to say, maybe?"

If Noah had taken even a moment to think about it, he wouldn't have had the nerve. As it was, though? Shane's smirk, his teasing, his long, lean body stretched out on the steps? Noah leaned forward so fast he almost lost his balance, and his lips landed somewhere on Shane's chin. Not a good kiss, but a kiss. He, Noah Reed, had just kissed Shane Black. Not on the mouth, unfortunately, but on the face, at least. His intentions had been bold enough, it was just his aim that needed work.

Noah pulled back, suddenly not cold anymore. Shane didn't

move at all. "Are you even gay?" Noah demanded. "I mean, okay, apologies if you aren't. You said that thing about Roman's assumption not being all that weird, and we spend quite a bit of time in your bed together, more than would be typical if one of us is straight, but, okay, maybe you're just really relaxed about stuff. I don't know. And apologies if you're gay but you just aren't interested. I mean, I get it. Tristan's beautiful, and he seems to really care about you, and I'm obviously not—" Noah waved a hand at himself, not really having the words to say all the things he was not. "I get it. I just—sorry. I apologize."

Shane was still for a while longer, then raised an eyebrow. "You know, that kind of self-doubt? It's really just a form of self-pity, or self-centeredness, isn't it? I mean—"

"Okay. That's funny. I get it. I deserve that. But, please, Shane. I'm going a bit crazy." He stopped, sighed, and said, "Obviously. I just really need—I don't know. Can you just tell me—anything? If you're straight, that'd be something I should know about. If you're just not interested, maybe you could—"

"Noah, stop."

Noah did, for a moment, but he couldn't maintain his control. "I just—" he started, and then Shane reached out and this time it was *his* hand on *Noah's* mouth, and the ability to even form words was completely erased from Noah's mind.

"Shhh," Shane whispered. "Everything's okay. Settle down."

"But—" Noah mumbled. But he stopped when Shane's hand didn't move away.

Shane nodded in approval, then frowned as if thinking about Noah's questions. "I don't think I'm gay," he said slowly, but before Noah's heart could break, he added, "not completely. I'm not that much of anything, really. I mean, I don't think about it too much. Sex, or any of that. But I've had sex with guys, and it was fine. Tristan and I used to mess around, and I liked it." He stopped as if waiting for Noah's reaction to his confession, but when he didn't get one, he continued. "I like you. We can do stuff if you want." And then bashful Shane was back for a moment as he said, "I'd like to. If you want."

"What kind of stuff?" Noah said, his words still muffled by Shane's warm hand.

"Any kind, I guess. What did you have in mind?"

Noah hoped his blush wasn't visible in the dim light, then wondered if Shane could feel the rising heat of Noah's face under his hand. Damn it. There was no way he could put any of that into words.

Shane slid his hand away from Noah's mouth, but didn't pull it back entirely. Instead, he drew it lower, down over Noah's jawline to his neck. Oh.

"Stuff like this?" Shane asked, and he guided Noah toward him as he leaned forward himself. They met in the middle, Shane's lips soft, their kiss a question.

Noah supposed he should have words. Some sort of witty repartee, maybe even, something sophisticated and urbane. Instead, he made a strange little whimpering sound and pushed for more. He wanted nudity, he wanted depravity, he wanted long, loving stares in between the bouts of perversion. Whatever Shane would give him, he would take.

But for right then? Oh, he wanted this kiss. His hands found their way to Shane's thighs, not as an advance but just because he needed to balance himself. But once they were there, he flattened them against the hard muscles beneath the denim, and he felt Shane shift in response. Noah shuffled closer without breaking the kiss, his cold, wet knees forgotten, until he was kneeling in the space between Shane's legs. Shane brought his thighs in closer, making Noah feel trapped in the best possible way, and Noah let his hands wander, up along Shane's strong arms, behind his neck, over his face, down to his chest.

He was tempted to go further. It wasn't like Shane was shy, was it? And apparently right then, Noah wasn't feeling too shy, either. But something slowed him down. What had Shane said?

Noah forced himself to pull away, at least a little. It wasn't like he couldn't dive back in at a moment's notice. "What did you mean?" he asked, his voice shakier than he'd expected. "When you said you aren't much of anything, and you don't think about sex? Like, you don't think about it at all?"

Noah kind of wished he hadn't said anything, or at least that he'd stayed close enough to not get such a clear view of the expression on Shane's face. As it was, though, he saw Shane look away, as if trying to escape from the question, and then look back, but with his eyes focused somewhere around Noah's ear.

"I think about it," he said. "Just not as much as some people, I guess. I mean—I don't know. It's not as a big a deal for me as it is for some people. That's all."

Noah tried to sort it out. Shane's kisses had been—god, had Noah been paying any attention to what Shane had actually been doing, or had he just been paying attention to himself, and to his own explorations of Shane's body?

Well, Shane had been kissing back, for sure. Noah would have noticed if he hadn't been at least *that* into it. "When you do think about sex," he asked, not sure if he wanted to know the answer, "do you think about guys? Or girls?"

Shane took a deep breath, then looked Noah in the eyes. "For the last couple days, I've been thinking about you."

And that was enough, surely. That had to be enough. But some aggravating little interrogator in Noah's brain made him ask, "What do you think about? What did you think about doing with me?"

It wasn't really a fair question. If Shane turned it around and wanted to know what Noah had thought about doing to *him*, Noah was pretty sure he'd melt right into the ground in a big pool of embarrassment. But Shane didn't turn it around. He just shrugged and said, "Being with you, I guess. Lying down with you, like we do in my room. You and me and Dodger. Maybe touching a bit more than we normally do—you and me, not Dodger for that part." He saw Noah's expression and seemed to interpret it pretty accurately. "But just because I didn't think about doing more doesn't mean I don't *want* to do more. I'm just telling you what I thought about so far. Maybe I just don't have a very good imagination, right? Maybe I just—" He stopped, and looked away again. "I like you," he said, his voice quiet. "I don't care what we do. It's all good."

Another chance for SmartNoah to step in and take what he could get. But CaringNoah was apparently still in charge, unfortunately. "What about with other people? Is this typical for you, or is it just me?" He made himself say it. "With Tristan—" Beautiful, perfect Tristan—"did you think about it with him?"

Shane was still for a moment. Far too still. Then he stood up so abruptly that Dodger's little head flopped a little and almost hit the step before the pup woke up enough to catch himself. "You're cold, right?" Shane said. "You want to come inside and warm up, or you want me to walk you to the bus stop?"

Two choices, just like Shane had given Roman that first night. *Tell me what you're doing here or fuck off.* Was Shane giving Noah a similar ultimatum? And if he was, how was Noah supposed to respond?

He probably wasn't too graceful as he rose to his feet, but he managed it. "I'm not that cold. And maybe I should get home and get some sleep. But, Shane? I like you too. A lot. I like you enough that I want to be sure you're not doing anything you don't want to do, just because you're a good guy."

Shane blinked once, then twice. Finally he said, "I'm really not that good of a guy, you know."

"I'll be the judge of that," Noah responded, and somewhere he found the courage to stretch up and give Shane a quick kiss. His instincts had apparently told him to react to an ultimatum by ignoring it; unfortunately, he couldn't really read Shane's expression to know whether his instincts were making good suggestions or not.

"So, you're going?" Shane asked. "I should walk you."

"You don't have to," Noah said. He wanted to stop whatever was happening and just make it crystal clear that—what? That he didn't care if he pushed Shane into something he didn't want to do? That Noah was delusional enough to think he actually had the influence to push Shane to do a goddamn thing?

"Noah?" Shane's voice was quiet, but impossible to ignore. Noah looked at him and waited for the verdict. "You're thinking too much, I think. I mean, your brain is great. It's excellent that you think things through. But some things you don't really need to think about all that much, you know?"

"The last time I didn't think things through, it didn't really go all that well."

Shane frowned at him. "You mean Roman? *Four years ago*? For four years, everything you've done, you've thought it all through before you did it?"

Noah didn't say anything, but apparently his silence was answer enough for Shane.

"Seriously?" Shane took a half-step backward and inspected Noah like he was an alien species. "Okay, obviously I'm nobody who should be offering you or anybody else advice on any damn thing." Then he stepped forward, even closer in to Noah than he'd been before. "So, it's not advice. It's just something to— something to think about, I guess."

And then he leaned in and kissed Noah, and there was nothing unsure about his lips or the hand that pulled their bodies together. There was nothing but warmth and pressure and the silky glide of their tongues, the rough friction of their bodies. Nothing but Shane and Noah, an island of heat in the cold night.

Shane pulled away far too soon, and when Noah's body unconsciously leaned after him, Shane gently pushed him back. "So, if you're going to think about something, think about that," he said. "Okay?"

Noah's lips felt swollen and he wasn't sure he could trust his voice, so he just nodded.

"Okay. So, I'll walk you to the bus stop now. And you'll go home, but you'll come back tomorrow, or the next day or whenever."

"Tomorrow," Noah practically gasped. He wasn't sure he was going to survive the night without contact, let alone another whole day. "I don't have classes until the afternoon. Can I come by in the morning?"

"To work? To go talk to people?"

"If you want." It wasn't like it would be appropriate to do what *Noah* wanted, not with the clinic full of people.

"Or maybe—" Shane frowned. "I might want to go talk to Raven. She's still in the hospital, last I heard, and I hate hospitals, but—it might be a good idea?"

"To see what she's going to do when she gets out? Where she's going to live with the kids?"

Shane shook his head. "No. But I think it might be a good idea to see who might have hated Andy enough to want to poison him."

Chapter Fourteen

IT WASN'T THE SMELL of hospitals that made Shane's skin crawl. It wasn't even the sick people. It was just the overall sense of authority, bureaucracy, unknowable rules and rituals. There was the strangest combination of feeling as if surveillance was on high alert, all focused on him, but also as if he was being ignored.

But it was easier to take when he had Noah beside him.

"Do you want me to wait outside?" Noah asked when they'd finally navigated their way to Raven's room.

"I don't think so. I mean, you saved her, right? She should at least meet you."

"But will she tell you what you want to know if a stranger is listening?"

"It's not like she's got a private room. With visitors and everything there's probably, like, ten other people in there. If she won't talk with strangers listening, she's not going to talk." And, really, it wasn't like Shane had a clear idea of what he was doing, anyway. It had seemed like a good idea the night before, when he'd been practically high on the adrenaline from getting away from the police station and then kissing Noah. But everything was different in the harsh daylight.

When Noah had come to find Shane at the clinic an hour or so earlier, there'd been no kissing, just awkward nods of greeting and an equally awkward conversation about their plans. They'd stood next to each other on the bus to the hospital, and sometimes their bodies had touched when they'd shuffled together to let other passengers get past, but each time, Noah had pulled away quickly.

It was confusing, and frustrating, and Shane didn't like it at all. The night before Noah had seemed so sure, and then become unsure so quickly, and now it seemed as if he was just as sure as he'd been to begin with, but in the opposite direction. Probably that was what happened when you thought things through like Noah did; you ended up making good decisions, but not ones that other people could really understand.

Shane poked his head through the open doorway of the hospital room and scanned the beds for Raven, trying to distract himself from thinking about Noah. There was something more important going on, something that maybe, just maybe, Shane could help with.

Raven was in the far bed, by the window, and the other three beds were surrounded by family and friends. Raven was alone, picking at her fingernails, but she smiled when she saw Shane.

"You're looking better," he said, which was probably

stupid, considering she'd been practically dead the last time he'd seen her.

"Feeling better," she agreed. "They say I can leave today, as long as I keep taking the pills and check in at the clinic."

"And the kids?" He regretted having asked the question as soon as he saw her expression.

"They're in a foster home. The social workers *say* it's temporary. They say as soon as I have somewhere to stay, I can have them back. But where the hell am I supposed to live?"

"There are shelters," Noah said, and Raven frowned in his direction.

"This is Noah," Shane said. "He's the one who called the ambulance for you."

"He called the *cops* on me," she retorted. "Sent the fucking social workers after my kids."

"You would have died without the ambulance," Shane said. Raven was tough, and there was no reason to pretend about anything. "Then the kids would have been in foster care forever, not just for a bit. So if he says there are shelters, you should at least listen."

She rolled her eyes at Shane, but that was all, and after a moment, Noah said, "I don't have a lot more information on that— I know more about the veterinary side of things, to be honest. But there are definitely shelters that take moms and kids. Programs to help out." He looked thoughtful. "And this situation has gotten some press. It was on the news two or three nights in a row. That might mean there'd be private people, or churches or charities or whatever, willing to step in and help you out. Lena—" He gave Raven an apologetic look and added, "she's a social worker, but I don't think she'd want to take your kids or anything. I think she'd want to help. And she's really good at publicity and networking and knowing who to reach out to for different things. I could ask her to talk to you, if you wanted."

Raven cut her eyes toward Shane. "Is he serious?"

"He knows what he's talking about; you should listen to him."

Raven looked Noah up and down, then raised her eyebrows at Shane. For someone who'd been almost dead a few days earlier, she seemed pretty damn active. "You're telling me he knows about being lied to by social workers, or losing your kids, or getting stuck in the system?"

Well, that was a good point, but Shane wasn't ready to give up yet. "He knows about *not* getting stuck in the system or losing your kids. He knows how to use all that stuff to help you, not get in your way."

"I'm not an expert," Noah said quickly. "I'm just saying I know someone who I think you can trust. She's helped Shane out, so far."

She'd helped Shane out. Strange how easy it was to suggest that Raven take someone's charity, and how hard it was to hear Noah point out that Shane had taken charity, too. Sure, Lena and Dr. Anderson might have done a good job of disguising it, but

Noah was right. The clinic didn't really need a night guard—it had gotten along just fine without one. And the job? He'd known from the start that it was charity, but he'd talked himself out of believing it.

But it was true. And Noah knew it. He knew Shane was a charity case, and of *course* he'd come to his senses and realized he didn't want to get any more involved with a loser who couldn't even look after himself.

"Who hated Andy?" Shane demanded. Too loud, too forceful, and Raven pushed back into her pillow, eyes wide. Damn it. Messing this up was just one more way Shane was pathetic.

He tried to sound calmer, more like a friend and less like an interrogator, when he added, "I'm wondering if it was deliberate. Someone trying to kill Andy, not trying to kill a random person."

"There was a lot of food in that container," Raven said after a pause, still looking like she was a bit afraid of Shane. "If someone was going after just Andy, they sure didn't care who else got hurt."

Which meant either Shane's theory was wrong, or they were dealing with an even bigger psycho than they'd thought. Both options were totally possible.

"It's just a guess," Shane said. "But it's something to check out, maybe."

"The cops asked me about that before, you know. What Andy had been up to, what enemies he might have had."

Of course they'd asked. They were assholes, but they were professionals. They knew their jobs, and Shane had been stupid to think he'd come up with a fresh idea they hadn't already considered. God, everything he did was such a waste of everybody's time.

But then Raven said, "I didn't tell them shit. I figured they were just trying to show that he was a bad guy or something, so nobody should care that he got murdered. They didn't explain it to me like you did."

Shane was pretty sure his explanation had been barely adequate, but he didn't think there was much point in saying so. Instead, he said, "So you didn't tell them anything, but—is there something to tell? Was Andy doing something that might have gotten him in trouble?"

Raven cast a doubtful look in Noah's direction before sighing and telling Shane, "He was trying to set up a business. You know, a way to support the family. It was really important to him that he take care of us, you know?"

Shane nodded. "What kind of business?"

Another pause, then she said, "Protection."

Shit. "Seriously? He was trying to set up a protection racket? That's not something an independent can usually pull off." Especially not an independent who looked as completely non-threatening as Andy had. "Was he working for somebody?"

"Not 'for'. 'With'. He had two guys—big guys, like you—

who did the muscle side of things. Or at least, they were going to, if it ever got that far. But I don't think it ever did. They just walked around with Andy and looked tough."

Two big guys plus Andy. It'd take quite a bit of poisoned fish to put three full-grown men out of service. So maybe Shane's theory was back in play. "Do you know who Andy was shaking down? Or where I can find these guys? What are their names?"

She shook her head. "I never met them. Andy didn't want me mixed up in any of that." She looked at Shane and said, "I actually suggested he ask you for help, but he didn't want to have anyone connected to the family to be part of the business. I don't know where he found the guys."

"Do you know where he was working? Most streets are already claimed, right?" Had Andy gone up against some organized crime group and lost? But they'd usually want their killings to be public enough to serve as a warning to others. Poison seemed too sneaky for mafia, whether Italian or Russian or any other kind.

"He said he found an opportunity," Raven said. "I don't know any other details."

Found an opportunity? "How long ago? When did this start?"

"About two months, maybe?"

An opportunity, a couple months earlier.

"There was—" Noah started, but then he stopped, looking doubtful.

"What?" Shane prompted. Noah was smart; if he had something to say, Shane should hear it.

"I just read about it in the paper. I don't know anything. I'm really just guessing what you're even talking about."

"What'd you read in the paper?"

"Back in the fall—September, maybe? A couple months ago, like Raven said. There was all that stuff about the Russian mafia? They hadn't thought they were active in Seattle, but then they found a cell, or whatever they're called, and made a bunch of arrests."

Yeah, Shane had heard a bit about that. "Not the top guys," he mused. "But a lot of street-level people, right?" Maybe enough to have left a few holes someone like Andy could fill, at least until the Russians got organized again.

Jesus. Russian mafia. This was so far out of Shane's league he didn't even know what game it was anymore. "If this is something that big, you're *out,* Noah. You're not fucking with them. You know that, right?"

"Jesus, Shane, if it's organized crime, you're out too. Right? You can't think you're going to take them on yourself."

"Not take them on, no. But I could still poke around a lit—
"

"No." Noah said it like he had some authority, some right to tell Shane what to do. But he didn't. Whatever had almost happened the night before? If that had happened, if they were—

whatever they'd be if it had happened—then maybe Noah could start making rules for Shane. But as it was?

"I'll decide," Shane said.

Noah gave him a frustrated look. "Does the Russian mafia use poison?" he asked. "I should call Brennan and tell him about this."

"Yeah, go running to him and let him make you feel safe," Shane said. He regretted the words, and the tone, as soon as he was done speaking. Was he jealous of *Brennan*, now? Was he that pathetic?

Noah frowned. "It's his job to make all of us feel safe. It's not about—"

"Andy wasn't fucking stupid," Raven interjected, and Shane and Noah both turned to look at her. "Seriously, you think he'd have messed with anyone big? As if! He might have stepped in to fill a gap or something, but he never would have taken them on directly. No way."

That all made sense, and left Shane feeling a bit stupid. He was getting too emotional about all this, letting the shit with Noah affect him way too much. "Okay," he managed, trying to collect his thoughts. "So if the Russians weren't mad at him, maybe it was one of the people he was shaking down. You're sure you don't know where he was setting things up? Did he ever bring home anything but cash when he went out? Ever mention—I don't know, things he'd seen that day, or anything?"

Raven frowned down at her lap, clearly trying to remember. Shane just hoped there would be some payoff for her efforts. "He complained a couple times about the construction on Twelfth Avenue," she finally said. "He said the sidewalk was blocked in a couple places. And I don't think he had any other reason to be over there, really."

Twelfth Avenue. Shane wasn't an expert, but he was pretty sure protection scams worked best in neighborhoods with a lot of recent immigrants, people who weren't sure how things were done in the States and would be more likely to pay instead of going to the cops. And Twelfth Avenue went right through Chinatown.

He had no idea of anyone in Chinatown sold fish and chips, but it was somewhere to start, at least.

"Do you have a picture of Andy?" Shane asked. He didn't really have a plan, but a picture might reasonably be part of it.

"Nothing printed. But I have some on my phone."

Of course she did. But Shane knew better than to ask to borrow the phone itself.

"Send them to me," Noah said calmly. Shane wanted to object, but wasn't sure how. So Raven and Noah exchanged whatever information it took to send a picture to somebody while Shane tuned out; if he ever had the money to get a phone, he'd worry about how to use it, but in the meantime, his didn't have any brainpower to spare. And he couldn't be distracted by Noah, either; there was just no point. He needed to focus on the few parts of his life that he might actually be able to control.

Someone had poisoned Andy. Andy had been trying to set up a protection racket. Shane could understand and maybe even forgive the person for doing what he could to get rid of a threat to his business, if it had only been Andy who'd been hurt. But Raven? Jayden and Jory, and Dodger? No one in the world could be more innocent than Jayden and Jory and Dodger. Whoever had hurt them needed to be dealt with, and Shane would do what he could to make sure that happened. Whatever else was going on in his life, this one thing would be taken care of.

*****

Noah had no idea what was going on. Well, everything on the surface was pretty clear. He and Shane were walking away from the hospital, with Andy's photos safe on Noah's phone and Shane charging along like a man on a mission. Yes, that was all straightforward. But what was going on underneath? What was Shane thinking, or feeling, about any damn thing?

The night before had started to seem like a dream, and one that had only happened in Noah's mind, not Shane's. Noah had been the only one who'd felt awkward that morning at the clinic, not knowing what sort of greeting was allowed. He'd been the only one struggling on the bus, fighting the urge to grab hold of Shane's hard body and start peeling clothes off both of them. And he was apparently the only one thinking about any of it now as they headed down the sidewalk toward wherever Shane was taking them.

God, *had* it been a dream? A lust-induced hallucination, wishful thinking turning into a disconnection from reality?

No, of course not. It was just that it hadn't been a big deal for Shane, and he had more important things to worry about now. Maybe later, if he got bored or something, he'd start thinking about Noah again. Or maybe he'd move on entirely.

If Noah hadn't hesitated, he'd have had a chance to—to what? To make a stronger impression, maybe, to somehow persuade Shane that they'd be good together. Or at least to create a more vivid memory for himself to use for comfort on cold winter nights.

As it was, though, he'd hesitated, Shane had called him on it, and now it was over.

"Where can we go to get that picture printed?" Shane asked. "I don't know how it works."

"I can e-mail it to myself and print it at home," Noah said. "Or at school. Or we could find a printing shop or something, if you want."

"Whatever's easiest."

"It'd be easiest to leave it on my phone, really, and just show it to people on the screen. I mean, who are you planning to show it to? Shouldn't we be calling Detective Brennan and giving him the new information? Then if he needs a picture of Andy, I can e-mail it to him."

"We're not telling Brennan," Shane said firmly.

Damn it, Noah had thought they were past that, at least until it had flared up again in the hospital room. "It's his job to look into all this. And you said he was good last night. Reasonable, or whatever. He believed us when we told him about Roman."

"There was something else going on there. He was *waiting* to hear Roman's name, practically. I don't know what that was about, but Brennan sure didn't think it was necessary to explain it to me. So I don't think I need to explain any of this to him."

"Damn it, Shane, you can't be petty about this! If there *is* something more going on with Roman, that's their business, just like the information about Andy is their business, because they're the damn police. Solving crimes is *their* job, not yours."

"Yeah, and they're doing a great fucking job. Jesus, they have the manpower to bust us for a little bottle of K, but how many people do they have working on a case where somebody actually died, and three people and a puppy almost did too? Don't pretend the cops care, Noah."

"No, nobody cares," Noah retorted. He knew he was being childish, but he couldn't stop himself. Or maybe he just didn't want to stop himself. "Brennan doesn't care, the other cops don't care, *you* don't care—"

"What? What do *I* not care about?"

"About *me*!" Damn it. Such a petulant baby.

But instead of looking annoyed, Shane just seemed confused. "You? What's wrong with you? I mean, what do you need?" The frustration he'd shown in the hospital was gone, replaced with concern. "If you need something, I can try to get it for you."

Well, Noah had started, so he'd damn well finish. "What if it's not a need so much as a want?" he asked. He sounded like he was looking for a fight, and maybe he was. "What if what I want is you?"

Shane stared at him for quite a while, then slowly said, "You want me... to do what?"

"Are you kidding me?" Noah tried to get himself under control, then abandoned the effort. "They wrote a damn song about it, Shane! I want you to want me! I mean, did you hit your head last night and get retrograde amnesia? Have you forgotten everything that happened?"

"Forgotten?" Shane still seemed confused. "No. But—you were just emotional or something, right? It doesn't have to be a big deal, Noah."

Well, now there were two of them who had no idea what they were talking about. "Emotional? I guess a little, yeah." If lust counted as an emotion. "But—are you saying—you think *I* want to forget about it? Is that what you think?"

"You were going to think about it, right? So—you thought about it. And then you came in this morning and you were just casual, so, yeah, I figured that meant you wanted to forget about it."

"I was not casual! I was—" Noah really wasn't sure he

wanted to say he'd been paralyzed by fear and self-consciousness, but what other words could he use? "I don't want to forget about it. I was just playing it cool because there were people around."

"Oh." Shane nodded slowly. "Okay, sorry. That makes sense. Dr. Anderson is going to help you get into vet school, right? You don't want her to think you're making bad choices about—"

"Stop." There was a strange sense of calm washing over Noah. He felt centered, as if the world had stopped spiralling out of control and was back to making sense. "I didn't want to put on a show in front of all the clinic people because I don't want to put on a show. But I'm not ashamed of wanting to be with you, and I'm not planning to hide anything from Dr. Anderson, on the off-chance that's she actually interested. I just felt self-conscious. You and I hadn't really settled anything last night, and I didn't want to fumble through it all with an audience. But I don't think you're a bad choice, Shane. Not at all."

"I can't help you with—"

"Maybe somebody can help *you*, for a change."

"I don't need your fucking charity!"

Noah actually stepped back, away from the re-emergence of Shane's frustration and anger. What the hell was going wrong now? "It's not charity. No more than it would be charity if you helped me with what I want. God, you know this, Shane! Is it charity when you kick people out of Tristan's apartment to keep them from taking advantage of him? No, it's just about being a friend. Isn't it? And that's all I'm saying to you. I'd like to be your friend. Honestly, I have no idea what I'd ever do to help you, other than carrying my damn cell phone around all the time, but if something came up, it wouldn't be charity for me to help you out, it would just be being friends." Shane didn't seem nearly as angry anymore, so Noah really, really should do the smart thing and shut up, but he kept going anyway. "And it's not charity when, or if, Detective Brennan helps. That's just him doing his job. You know?"

Shane clearly didn't like the idea of taking the conversation in that direction. "Can we go back to the part *before* you said you wanted to help me? The part where you just wanted me to want you?"

"Okay," Noah said carefully.

"Okay," Shane agreed. Then he shrugged. "I want you. I don't know if it's exactly the kind of 'wanting' you want from me, but it's what I've got. I like you, I want you, sex is good, stuff that's like sex but isn't actually sex is good, just lying around together is good—I want all of that. Okay?"

"Yes." Noah said, and the world stopped spiralling again. "That sounds good. I want all of that too."

"Starting now?" Shane asked, but he didn't wait for an answer. Right there on the sidewalk, with half the world walking by and giving them curious stares, Shane put his hand on Noah's neck and held him still while Shane shuffled forward. "This is okay?" Shane asked, but again, there was no time for Noah to respond before Shane's lips found his, and at that point Noah's powers of speech were pretty well done away with.

Shane guided them over to the brick wall they'd been standing next to and gently shoved Noah against it. The wall at his back, Shane's arms on either side, and Shane's body, lean and hard and strong, pinning him in place. It was absolutely perfect.

Noah let go of his inhibitions, lost his awareness of where they were and who might be seeing them. He just didn't care anymore. He didn't care about anything but Shane, and the way their bodies seemed to melt together as their lips and tongues joined.

It wasn't until an unfamiliar male voice said "Hell, yeah," and another said "Truly, we live in a marvelous age," that Noah came back to himself enough to realize they had an audience.

"Don't let us interrupt," the middle-aged man said from his spot a few feet away. "In fact, we're meeting friends from out of town here in just a few minutes, so if you could carry on, we'd really appreciate it. A great way to show them the beauties of our fair city."

"You're so inappropriate," the man's partner said, but he kept their fingers laced tightly together.

Shane shifted a little, just enough so his back was blocking most of the mens' view, but Noah got his hands between them and gently held Shane away. "Not the time or place," he managed to say.

"So, when and where?"

For someone who apparently didn't think about sex very often, Shane was certainly good at focusing on it once he got going.

"I'm not sure," Noah admitted. "But, honestly—I want it, and you want it? So we'll make it happen."

"Soon," Shane growled.

"Soon," Noah promised. He would damn well make sure of it.

Chapter Fifteen

SHANE KNEW AS SOON as he walked into the place. He'd already found seven other businesses in the neighborhood where the owners recognized Andy's face with a mix of fear and anger, but this place was different. Something about the way the man behind the counter tracked every move Shane made, his eyes narrowed with hostility that Shane hadn't yet done anything to deserve. It was a kitchen supply store, lots of steamers and woks and other stuff Shane had no idea about, not a sign of fish or chips anywhere in the place, but still, Shane knew.

And it made sense, really. Why poison somebody with a product that might be traced back to you when it would be so easy to buy something at a neighboring shop and poison *that*? Drive it over to the place you were supposed to be meeting your harasser, give it to him as a peace offering, and let nature take its course. A different kind of man might not have eaten food provided by a hostile stranger, but Andy hadn't been that bright, and he'd always been hungry. Whether the poisoner had known that or had just gotten lucky was a detail.

Still, a suspicious and hostile vibe from the owner wasn't enough to really be sure of anything, so Shane stepped up to the counter, ignoring the kitchenware and keeping his gaze locked on the proprietor.

"What do you want?" the man demanded, just a trace of some sort of Eastern European accent in his voice.

"I'm here for the payment," Shane said. "Andy sent me."

The man snorted. "Nobody sent you. That useless shit is dead."

"Oh, you saw that on the news? Too bad. There's a new Andy, and he's the one who sent me, and he wants his payment."

"I already told the animals who work for the old Andy— I'm not paying."

Damn it, the guy had guts. Shane forced himself to remember Jadyn and Jory, sick almost to death and then locked away in foster care because this asshole had killed their stepfather and nearly killed their mother. This guy wasn't a hero, and Shane wasn't going to let him get away with hurting the kids, or Dodger. "You know what happens if you don't pay."

"And do you know what happens if you keep bothering me?" The man's gaze, the quiet confidence in his expression was enough. Shane knew. He could act on this. He'd walk out now, come back later with some gasoline or something and burn the bastard out. Maybe he'd talk to Trey and some of the other guys who weren't afraid of getting a little dirty and they'd set something up. It could all be taken care of.

But Noah.

Noah wanted Shane, and Noah wanted safety. He wanted things done a certain way. So Shane pushed a little harder. "If I keep bothering you?" Shane echoed. "What, seriously? You're taking credit for Andy eating some bad fish? No way. Andy got unlucky, that's all."

"You're so sure about that?"

"You're telling me you poisoned Andy? Bullshit."

There was a moment when the man almost said it. If Shane had been better at his job, if he'd pushed different buttons, or pushed them just a bit harder, or *something*, the guy would have spilled. But Shane had no idea what to say, and then the moment was gone.

"Get out of my store," the man said.

Shane stood still, trying to think. Push harder? Walk away and come back later with a better plan? What would Noah want him to do?

Then he noticed the trickle of sweat running down the man's neck. It wasn't that hot in the store. "Andy was a friend of mine," Shane said slowly. "I'm taking a collection to pay for his funeral, and to help out his girl and her kids. You want to make a donation? I'm thinking a couple grand would do. This time."

"Get out of my store and don't come back." The man's voice was tight, ready to break.

"Okay," Shane agreed, and he took a step backward without taking his eyes from the man's face. "I'll leave. I'll go outside, and I'll call the fucking cops, and I'll tell them they need to come down here and talk to you about what happened to Andy. That sound good to you? You got anything to hide in that area? Anything that might be worth a couple grand for me to keep quiet about?"

Another moment, and Shane could practically see the store owner making his decision. Then he moved quickly, darting his hand under the counter and yanking a shiny black handgun up from its hiding spot. He pointed it at Shane, held in two hands, shaking a little but not backing down. "You pushed your way in here attacked me," he said, and his eyes were blazing. "This will be self-defense."

The hard part was that it wasn't that far from the truth. This guy was defending his store the only way he could, once he'd decided not to go to the cops. Yeah, this was a logical thing for the guy to do, but Shane didn't feel like dying just because he'd wanted to play detective. "You're pulling a gun on me?" he said a little too loudly. He took a step backward, not that an extra few feet would mean anything if bullets started flying. "That's a bad idea, man."

"It's a perfect idea," the man replied. His confidence was clearly building. "Your friend tried to push me around, and I did what I had to. You're trying to push me around, and now—"

That was when they both heard the crash from the back of the store. The front door was yanked open at the same time. "Seattle PD," Detective Brennan said. His gun was pointed at the store owner and he had a sort of action pose going on in the doorway. "Drop your weapon."

"This hoodlum attacked me!" the storekeeper yelled.

"Drop your weapon!" Brennan ordered, his voice harder now.

There was a moment when Shane was pretty sure the man was going to start firing, with the first bullet cutting through Shane's chest and finding his heart. He could almost feel it, the way it would be more shock than pain, and then, so quickly, nothing at all. He could feel it, but he didn't want it, not now when things were finally starting to work out.

"Drop the weapon," another voice said, this one from the doorway to the back of the store, and the storekeeper whirled toward it.

Shane took the chance to duck behind a display shelf, and he looked over at Brennan, expecting the crack of a police revolver. But it didn't come. The storekeeper had turned his gun toward the back of the store, pointing it in the direction of Brennan's partner, and Brennan wasn't taking him down?

It made no sense, but it appeared to be true. "We don't want this to go bad," Brennan said, his voice calmer than it had been while the gun was still pointed at Shane. "But we need you to drop your weapon, sir. That's the only way for this to go, now."

A moment of frozen time, and then the man exhaled a long, shuddering breath and set the gun down on the counter.

More yelling, then, more commands being barked as the man was dealt with, and Shane sank down to the floor, his back against a shelf of assorted teapots, and stared as it all happened. He'd done that. He'd let Noah convince him to call Brennan, shared his plan with Brennan, and agreed to wear a wire. A fucking wire. He, Shane Black, was a fucking narc, helping the cops catch and arrest a poor guy who'd only been doing what he thought he had to do in order to protect his business.

"He poisoned the kids," Noah said from somewhere nearby, and Shane turned to see him crouched down next to the same shelf full of teapots. He was ignoring the police actions, his eyes big and round and fixed firmly on Shane. "He poisoned Raven and Dodger. He'll get a lawyer and all the stuff you know will come out at the trial, and they'll figure out what's fair."

Noah had been listening in the police van just outside; he'd heard what the man had said. Shane shook his head. "I'm not sure it's enough, really. He could have just been making stuff up to make me go away."

"Brennan says it'll be enough for a search warrant, and for them to know where their investigation should be focused. This is way more than they had before; this is something they can build a case around."

And all because Shane had helped them out. He'd helped the damn police.

"I'm really proud of you," Noah said. "No, not proud, because that sounds like—I don't know, like I own you or something. I'm really impressed, maybe. How's that?"

"You can be proud if you want to be," Shane said. He didn't mind the idea of being owned by Noah; he didn't mind it at all.

Noah turned and slumped down beside Shane and he took Shane's hand and laced their fingers together. "I'm proud, then," he said. "You did what you had to do to keep people safe. And you were brave, and smart. Yeah, I'm proud of you."

Shane wasn't proud of himself. But somehow, that didn't seem to matter all that much, not when Noah was sitting beside him, their shoulders pressed warmly together, their thighs lined up, their hands entwined.

"And I talked to Brennan about Roman," Noah added. "We had some time to chat while you were out doing his job for him." A gentle smile to show that Noah was echoing Shane's opinion, not his own. Then he said, "He was a bit sketchy on the details, but I'm pretty sure the ketamine was already catalogued as police evidence, and they were trying to figure out how it got back out on the street. And Roman's dad's a cop. Seriously, Shane, this could be a pretty big thing for them. If Roman's dad stole it from the evidence lock-up and then Roman stole it from his dad? It's pretty huge. And you were part of helping them solve that, too."

Well, Shane didn't have nearly the same mixed feelings about that situation. One, he hadn't helped the cops on purpose, so that was okay. And two, Roman was an asshole who'd messed with Noah. He deserved what he got, and what his crooked cop father got, and whatever other bad things happened to him, ever. He shouldn't have tried to hurt Noah.

Shane shook his head. It had only been a few days since he'd found Raven and the kids, and hardly any longer than that since he'd met Noah. Not even a week. But it definitely felt like something old had ended, and something new had begun. Something rotten and useless was finished with, and something fresh and new was growing in its place. He could learn some new rules, maybe, a slightly different way of looking at the world, and the police. Or at least some of them.

"You want to get out of here?" he asked Noah. "We could find our time and our place."

Noah's smile was sweet and a little bit shy. "Sounds good," he agreed.

They heaved themselves to their feet, then stepped aside as Brennan's partner guided the handcuffed shop owner out of the store.

"You okay?" Brennan asked Shane. Shane tried to pull his hand away from Noah's, tried to protect Noah from having his reputation damaged in front of someone he obviously respected, but Noah hung on tight.

"He's fine," Noah said firmly. "But we're both pretty tired. Is it okay if we head out now?"

Brennan nodded. "Stop off at the van to return the wire. I've already got your affidavits signed. I think we're good for tonight, at least. But we'll need to stay in touch." He glanced at Noah, then gave Shane a longer, harder look. "You did good work here tonight. Good work the last few days. This wouldn't have been solved without your help, son. Thank you."

Shane knew he should be filled with disgust. The thanks of a police officer were an insult to anyone who valued their freedom. But instead of growling a response, he just nodded. He'd heard what Brennan had said, and he'd acknowledged it. Didn't necessarily mean he believed it. But he'd think about it, at least. And if he ran into too much trouble figuring it out, he could maybe ask Noah for a little help.

Feral

Chapter Sixteen

"WHAT DOES IT MEAN?" Noah asked. He'd already gotten to live out his fantasy of tracing Shane's tattoo with his fingers, and then his lips and tongue, but he found that the physical intimacy wasn't enough to satisfy him. He wanted to know Shane's brain as well as his body.

They'd come back to the clinic after the kitchen shop, managed to more-or-less behave themselves as Noah told the staff about Shane's heroics and Shane played with Dodger and pretended he wasn't listening, and then the staff had left and Noah'd had another bout of shyness. Shane *said* he wanted Noah, but it made no sense, and Shane was so willing to sacrifice himself, and he'd almost been *shot* that night, so the emotional trauma of that event might have been enough to affect Shane's decision making, and it was really pretty good just being friends, and really scary to think about jeopardizing that with an ill-fated attempt at something more—

And then Shane took off his shirt. Not just the hoodie, but the T-shirt underneath it. Right there in the hallway of the clinic, hidden from the street but still a public space, and Shane was half-naked. Noah stared at the beautiful, defined muscles in front of him and lost his ability to think at all.

"The tape they used from the wire had something weird on it," Shane said casually. He gestured at a couple little red marks on his chest. "It's itchy."

Itchy. That was a word that meant something to people with functioning brains. But Noah wasn't really part of that group right then.

"So I'm just going to have a quick shower, if that's okay." And now, sweet Jesus, Shane's hands were on the button of his jeans. "Wash the cop off me in case I'm allergic."

Noah managed to flop his head a little and Shane apparently understood that as agreement.

So Shane had showered, and when he came out of the bathroom he was wearing sweatpants but still no shirt and Noah's brain, which had started working at least a little, short-circuited again. "You want to come in?" Shane prompted, and Noah stumbled into Shane's room and practically collapsed onto the bed. "You okay?" Shane asked.

Noah didn't answer right away, since his mouth seemed to be working about as well as his brain, and Shane lowered himself to the mattress and looked at him with gentle concern. "Tough day? We can just—"

And that was when Noah finally found a little bodily autonomy. Sure, his hand shot out toward Shane's chest in a way that probably seemed more like an attack than a gesture of affection, but Shane didn't flinch away. And somehow touching Shane, letting the warmth of his skin seep into Noah's chilled hands, calmed Noah down a little. "I'm fine," he managed to say. He flattened his palm over Shane's pectoral muscle, then looked up nervously, expecting Shane to be looking shocked and about to proclaim that Noah had misunderstood everything and had to leave.

But Shane just gave him an encouraging smile. "Are you nervous? We don't have to—"

And again Noah interrupted, this time by launching himself sideways in a disorganized sprawl of limbs that fate generously allowed to land in more or less their intended positions. And then, on his knees, straddling Shane's lap, their faces so close Noah could feel the air of Shane's exhalation of surprise, Noah got to examine the tattoo.

No texture, at least none that he could feel with his fingers. And no color, just black ink against warm brown skin. Almost disappointing that there was no taste when Noah kissed and then licked it, but Noah couldn't feel too bad about that when Shane leaned his head away, giving Noah more room and encouraging his explorations.

"What does it mean?" Noah asked.

Shane didn't answer right away, not until Noah had pulled

his head back and looked him in the eyes. "It's a family thing, kind of," Shane said.

And that was too much of an opportunity to pass up. "Family? Where are they? Around here?"

But Shane shook his head. He kissed Noah's mouth, and for a while Noah figured the conversation must be over and had trouble really making himself care, but then Shane leaned back on the bed and stretched his long, beautiful arm over to catch one of the straps of the backpack resting against the wall. As far as Noah could tell, that pack carried all Shane's worldly possessions, so the part of his brain that wasn't wondering if it held condoms and lube was curious about what else might be in it.

He was a bit surprised when Shane pulled out a little wooden figure, one that fit Shane's hand from wrist to fingers. Probably just Noah's over-sexed brain that saw the thing as phallic, since it had a wide, pointy pair of wings sprouting from it near the top. "A totem pole?" he asked, and immediately felt like an idiot. Of course it was. Shane's tattoo wasn't a monster, it was a curved representation of a totem pole. Noah squinted at the object in Shane's hand. The tattoo was a version of *this* totem pole. "It's connected to your family?"

Shane shrugged. "Maybe. My mom was—I don't know. Damaged, I guess. She lied a lot, to herself more than to anyone else. So I don't know if it's true. But she said she was Native Amer—well, Native Canadian. First Nations, she said they're called up there. And one summer, right before she left, we went on a road trip, up across the border. She had a boyfriend who was paying for it—I can't remember his name, but he was a nice guy. We went way up the coast, and took a ferry, or maybe two. I can't remember the details. But we got to this place called Haida Gwaii. She said she was Haida, and this was her home."

Shane kept his gaze on the miniature totem pole as he spoke. "It was the most beautiful place I'd ever seen. Trees and ocean and rocks and—everything just felt really *alive*, you know? Like there was just so much more greenness there than in the city, like even the rocks up there must be living." He was silent for a moment, clearly lost in his memories, then shrugged. "The people were really nice, but they'd never heard of my mom, or the people my mom said she was related to. They tried to help, and they said some of their history had been lost, for sure, so if my mom's people had left a long time ago they might have come from there, or from a village out on one of the other islands that got shut down, or they might have been going by different names or whatever." Another shrug. "Like I said, they were nice. But probably my mom had just made it up. I mean, if you saw pictures of the place, you'd want to make up a story that said you had ties to it, you know? It's that beautiful."

"But you kept the totem pole. Even though you don't think she's really from there?"

"This old guy up there—" Shane broke off, picked at one of the bracelets on his wrist, and then said, "He was a good guy. That's all. He really believed Mom's story, or at least was nice enough to pretend really well. He called me 'little brother', and he said I could learn to carve the totem poles like he did, if I wanted. We only stayed for a few days, because my Mom got all worked up about nobody being able to give her the proof she wanted, but before we left the old guy gave me that. He said he made it just for me."

"And you got it tattooed on your neck?"

"Not then. I was just little, then. Eight or nine, maybe. Nobody's going to ink up a little kid. But later, yeah. I got robbed, and they took my pack, and I realized that the only thing I'd really miss was this. So I tracked the thieves down and got it back, then I took it to a girl I know who does good ink, and she put it on me permanent. So nobody can take it, now."

It was probably the best explanation of a tattoo Noah had ever heard, even if it did make him want to cry a little for a couple different versions of younger Shane. "Your mom left shortly after the trip?"

Another long pause, another shrug, and then Shane said, "I guess. She just didn't come home one night. She left all her stuff behind, so, you know, that didn't—it didn't look too good. But maybe she just wanted a totally fresh start. It wasn't like she had anything really valuable to take with her, so if somebody gave her a good chance at something? Sure, she might have just gone with them."

Noah tried to let the information just settle in, tried not to analyze any of it or allow the conclusions to form in his brain, but he couldn't seem to hold them off. Shane's mother had not come home one night. So either something bad had happened to her, or something good had happened to her. And Shane wanted to believe it had been something good, even if that meant he had to classify himself in with all the rest of the "nothing valuable" that she'd left behind. "How long ago was that?"

"A while. Ten years, maybe?"

Noah wanted to ask whether she'd contacted him at any point in that decade, but he was pretty sure of what the answer was, and it was too cruel to make Shane admit it. So instead, he pushed Shane back on the bed so he was lying flat and then lay down with him, half on top, half beside, and nestled his face into Shane's neck. "Where'd you live after she left?"

"I stayed there for a while. In the apartment. That's where she'd come back for me, you know? But I couldn't pay the rent, so the landlord called the cops or whoever, and they put me in a foster home. I moved around a bit after that."

"Were—" Damn it, was Noah trying to comfort *himself* with this question? Probably, but he asked it anyway. "Were any of them nice? The foster families?"

"They were all okay, mostly. Just—you know. Not a lot of money, and not a lot of—I don't know, time, or patience or whatever? And some of the other kids were a bit rough sometimes. But the last one was good."

"Yeah? Who was that with?"

"Uncle Davey and Aunt Trish. They weren't real family,

but they liked it when the kids called them that."

"How old were you when you got to them?"

"Thirteen, maybe? I went to ninth grade when I was living with them."

"Wait. You said they were your last ones. So you went to all of high school with them, didn't you?"

"Nah." Shane sounded pretty unconcerned with the whole situation and his body was still relaxed, so Noah tried to loosen his own muscles up and concentrate on listening. Listening and snuggling. "They had too many kids," Shane said. "The rules are there's supposed to be a bedroom for each foster kid, but they had kids of their own, *plus* some other foster kids, so it was always kind of a game—shuffling the real kids out of the bedrooms when the social workers came by, then shuffling them back in once the visit was over. There wasn't much room, and Aunt Trish was kind of—she was kind of tense. So I started sleeping other places, just so there'd be more room. But I didn't really go to school, and the workers got all upset about that and started saying they were going to cut off the money if I didn't start going to school, and that made Aunt Trish even edgier, so I stayed away more, and didn't go to school at all, and—" He shrugged. "That was that. The social workers stopped paying, so Aunt Trish didn't want me around at all. Uncle Davey would still come find me sometimes, check up on me, throw a little work my way, even. But then he got caught and sent to jail, so—that was that."

Noah's brain was swimming. He had too many questions,

but he sensed that he'd asked a lot already, and at some point Shane was going to stop talking. So he just said, "I'm glad you're here now. With me."

Shane smiled, then, sweet and real, and dragged Noah up his body so they could kiss. "I'm glad, too," he said, and he ran his hands down over Noah's sides to sneak in under the fabric at his waist and find bare skin. "It's pretty warm in here," he said. "You want your shirt off?"

Well, a significant part of Noah certainly did. It wanted all of their clothes off, and probably burned or otherwise disposed of so he and Shane would be trapped in that room together forever, naked. But what he wanted wasn't the most important thing right then, and he was pretty sure Shane was making the offer on Noah's behalf, not his own. "Soon," he said. "But we have lots of time, right? We don't need to rush anything."

"You sure?" Shane asked, and there was something in his voice that *made* Noah sure.

"Yeah. We can just hang out, okay?" He leaned down and kissed Shane, then felt the pull of the tattoo, drawing his lips toward it. "Well, maybe hang out and make out? A bit?"

"A bit," Shane agreed. "Yeah. Okay. That sounds good."

It sounded good, and it felt good, and it *was* good. Noah nestled in next to Shane, and they were warm and comfortable together. Dodger joined them for a while and tried to burrow a place for himself between Shane's and Noah's ribs, but Noah didn't let him in and even soft-hearted Shane eventually lifted the pup over to his other side. "He's fine over there," Shane said, as if trying to reassure Noah rather than himself.

"There are dogs that aren't allowed on beds at all, you know," Noah said, and was rewarded with such a look of shock and outrage that he couldn't control his grin. "It's a form of abuse, I'm sure."

"Damn right," Shane growled, and he pulled Noah closer for a kiss-based reward.

Noah let himself be manhandled. Hell, if he was being honest, it was a pretty huge turn-on, having Shane drag him around like a toy. Shane was big and strong, and he was Noah's. Shane wanted to protect everybody; Noah just wanted to protect Shane.

He wasn't sure what their future would hold, wasn't sure if they'd be together forever. But even if they ended up apart, he wanted to be one of the good memories in Shane's life, not one of the too-common bad ones. He'd be Haida Gwaii, peaceful and full of life, or the old man up there who'd given Shane his totem pole. Hell, he'd even be Tristan, not sleeping with Shane anymore but still his friend, still looking out for him.

Or, even better? He shifted a little, rolling against Shane's thigh. Even better, he'd be Shane's forever. And they'd take care of each other for their whole lives.

Epilogue

"IT'S A GOOD HOUSE for a dog," Noah said. He was probably trying to be reassuring. "And it's been too long since we had one. Sarah's probably going to try to steal Dodger, so—keep an eye on that. If she gets him out of the room, she'll hide him and pretend he's lost or something. She's pretty sneaky."

"Your sister isn't going to steal my dog."

"Not as long as you're careful," Noah agreed. Then they stepped past the tall hedge that had been blocking their view and he nodded at a two-story house, kind of old-fashioned but still in good shape, and said, "The back yard's totally fenced. We can check the gate before we go in; we've probably gotten pretty careless about leaving it open, since we don't have a dog anymore, but once that's done, it's Dodger's playpen. He can just run around and check it out."

The house had wide steps leading to a front porch that probably should have seemed welcoming, but the whole place looked like a trap to Shane. Like it was *too* welcoming, or something. Why was the house trying so hard? What did it have to hide?

But Noah was already on his way up the concrete walk and Dodger was pulling on his leash, trying to follow. If Noah and Dodger were going to be trapped, then Shane might as well be trapped too. So he trudged up behind them.

There was a moment of hope when Noah turned at the bottom of the steps instead of going right up, but he was just going around to check on the gate. As if he actually thought Shane was going to let Dodger loose in the backyard! No, Dodger was going to be within easy grabbing distance for the entire damn visit, ready for a quick escape as needed.

"Shane," Noah said quietly. Shane had been following him at a bit of a distance, but now Noah had stopped walking and Shane caught up to him. They were in a sheltered spot between the tall hedge and the corner of the house, the wooden gate in front of them, a tree blocking the view from the street. Noah shook the gate to be sure it was securely closed, and then his fingers were cool when as took Shane's hand. "This is where I had my first kiss," Noah said.

Hmmm. Shane had found himself increasingly interested in Noah's kisses over the past few weeks as they'd gotten to know each other. Kisses and all the good stuff that sometimes came after kisses. "With who?"

"Nathan—" Noah's eyes widened. "Nathan—somebody.

Oh my god, I honestly can't remember his last name! He lived over by the school, he had blond hair that was always a bit too long. We played soccer together. What the hell was his last name?"

"You're getting old." Shane shifted around so Noah was between him and the wall, and then he waited.

Not for long. Noah tightened his fingers, tugged on Shane's hand just a little, and that was enough of a sign. Shane wasn't sure what the rules were for making out at someone's family's house, but Noah would know, and he seemed okay with this.

So Shane shuffled closer, let their bodies line up, and leaned in. Just enough weight to make Noah feel him, enough to pin him against the wall without squishing him flat. "Were you standing like this?" Shane asked.

Noah's eyes were wide in the way that always sent a message straight to Shane's dick. "Yeah," he whispered. "Our heads were probably a foot or so lower, but—"

Shane caught Noah's mouth with his own. He didn't care a whole lot about Nathan whoever, wasn't jealous of some kid from years ago. But Nathan wasn't there and Shane was, and Noah liked being kissed when he was standing against this wall, so Shane's role was clear.

He'd gotten pretty good at kissing Noah. Not that they hadn't been fine at the start, but he knew more, now. He knew about the sensitive spot on Noah's ribs, how brushing it just right made Noah's whole body sag with pleasure, but how touching it too lightly was an aggravating tickle and pressing it too hard didn't do a thing. He knew Noah's rhythms, knew he pushed with his forehead when he needed a tiny break, with his chin when he wanted a longer one. Usually he wanted the longer ones because he had something to say, and usually whatever he said was something Shane wanted to hear. It all worked out pretty well, as long as Shane was paying attention. And he made sure he always was.

Shane was just starting to feel the warmth of Noah's body soaking through their layers of clothes when the chin-push came and Shane obediently pulled an inch or two away. "We have to go inside," Noah said. He sounded a bit breathy, but not completely out of control yet. Unfortunately.

"We could say we missed the bus," Shane suggested, and trailed a line of kisses down along Noah's jaw. He didn't think he was actually going to get his way, but even a few more moments of peace would be something. "Maybe it broke down or something."

Noah huffed out a laugh and pushed Shane further away. "The bus didn't break down." His hands were still on Shane's chest and Shane leaned in a little, letting Noah hold some of his weight.

"Maybe there was an emergency at the clinic," he tried. "And you had to stay and help out."

"It's Sunday night. The clinic isn't even open."

"For an emergency it would be."

"There was no emergency at the clinic." Noah gave him a quick kiss. "My mom's really looking forward to meeting you. And so's Sarah, in her own way. We have to go inside."

"Maybe a dinosaur came to life—"

"A dinosaur didn't come to life," Noah said firmly, and this time he pushed Shane further away, then took his hand. "I want you to meet my family, Shane. Come inside."

It was what Noah wanted. So Shane let himself be led back along the walkway, with Dodger pulling happily on the leash, looking forward to his next adventure.

There was a woman looking out through the window by the front door. Older than Shane had expected, and way too put-together looking, wearing a dress that made him think might have worn it to church that morning. But she had Noah's warm eyes and they brightened just like his did when she saw them coming.

She pushed the door open as they were climbing the stairs. "I thought you might have missed the bus." But she just sounded gently concerned, not as if she was scolding them.

Noah squeezed Shane's hand. "Nope. Although we were slowed down a little when a dinosaur came to life."

"The challenges of modern travel," she said solemnly, then smiled at Shane.

It was almost too much. She looked so trusting, so open, so damn much like her son, and Shane was suddenly terrified again. He wasn't good enough for Noah, he wasn't good enough for this woman, or this house, or this neighborhood. They were going to trust him and he was going to mess it all up and ruin their perfect lives.

But Noah's fingers stayed tight around his, and the woman reached out and took his other hand, gripping the handle of

Dodger's leash at the same time. "I'm Shelly, and I'm so happy to meet you. Please, come inside."

Shane was strong. They couldn't hold him here, not if he didn't want to stay.

But Noah was looking at him, face full of pride and affection, and Shane couldn't let him down. "Thank you," he managed to say. And then he let himself be pulled inside.

Coming Soon

Lap Dog
The Shelter Series, Book Two

Chapter One

"What the hell are we doing here?" Micah hissed, looking around with a mix of disgust and apprehension on his face.

Tristan Beck frowned at him. Micah was a friend, but that didn't mean Tristan approved of all his decisions. No more than Micah approved of all of Tristan's. "We're here for Shane. It's his thing—be nice!"

"In what possible world are we living, when Shane Black's 'thing' is a fucking Puppy Parade?"

"It's a *Christmas* Puppy Parade," Tristan said, trying to pretend that made it all more understandable somehow. He looked out at the bewildering scene in front of him: Dogs of all shapes and sizes, most in some sort of festive costume, milling about a park lined with booths selling a variety of dog items. Somehow, it was a fundraiser for the veterinary clinic where Shane worked, but Tristan wasn't quite sure of the details. He'd come to show his support, and he'd probably end up buying something for a dog he didn't even own, just because it seemed like the thing to do. That was all he knew.

And then Shane himself was coming over, Dodger trotting happily beside him. The little dog had probably doubled in size in the last month or so, but he could still be easily scooped up with one arm, and absolutely expected the treatment whenever he met a friend. Now, seeing Tristan, he gave a happy yip and tugged at his leash, almost shaking his Santa hat free in his enthusiasm. At least seeing the pup gave Tristan a direction for his inevitable consumerism—he'd buy the little dog a Christmas present from one of the booths. Hopefully the clinic got a cut of the profits or something.

He crouched to greet Dodger and smiled up at the dog's owner. Shane had his own Santa hat on, perched at a jaunty angle that would have been enough to make most men look effeminate. If Tristan had tried it he knew he'd have looked like the twinkiest twink to ever twink down the streets of Twinksville. But somehow on Shane, the hat, even slanted as it was, seemed masculine. Macho, practically. All just part of the Shane mystique, Tristan figured.

"Thanks for coming, guys," Shane said as Tristan stood up.

Shane didn't lean in for the hug or kiss that he would have offered just a month or two earlier, and Tristan tried not to miss it. Shane had a boyfriend now, and Noah seemed happy to believe that Shane had come to him as something damn close to a virgin.

Or at least happy to believe that Shane wasn't still friends with someone he used to fuck through the mattress on a fairly regular basis.

Tristan was pretty sure that if he ever got a serious boyfriend he'd pull all the same defensive bullshit Noah was working on, so he tried not to bust the guy's balls about it. And he tried not to miss Shane's more physical greetings.

"It's a great event," Tristan said. He actually meant it. The whole scene was strange, hard to understand, totally foreign to his traditional view of the world—but, still, great. "I think the pugs dressed as elves are going to have to come home with me. Do you guys offer gift wrapping?"

"You don't even want to hear how much that lady charges for her dogs," Shane told him. "Unless you've got savings I don't know about, they're out of your league."

Tristan adopted a lofty tone as he said, "How disappointing," and was ready to move on.

But Micah had been quiet for too long, and now he chipped in with, "Maybe you could get one of your clients to buy them for you. You're running out of room for storing the rest of their crap."

From someone else, it might have been innocent. It wasn't like Tristan ever hid the way he earned his living: he was a whore, and a damn good one, and his clients expressed their complete satisfaction with gifts as well as cash. Nothing he was ashamed of, and if someone else, like Shane, had made the comment, Tristan would have laughed it off. But from Micah?

"I guess you've got the right system," Tristan said. "Better to spend all your money on shit to smoke or shoot into your veins, right? It's so bourgeois to accumulate material goods."

"Okay," Shane said quickly. "Not the best conversation for a happy, family-time Puppy Parade. Right?"

Tristan looked at Micah, and Micah looked back at him, long enough for the truce to be declared and approved. This was Shane's thing, after all. So Tristan said, "Puppy Parades? *So* bourgeois."

And Micah said, "The proletariat shudders and cries in despair."

Shane just shook his head. "I never have any idea what you two are talking about when you get going."

"That's because you, my friend," and Micah stretched up far enough to throw an arm at least part of the way across Shane's shoulders, "are a true member of the proletariat."

"Salt of the earth," Tristan agreed.

"Okay," Shane said, clearly tired of the topic. "That's great. But do either of you know the guy over there in the black Benz?"

All the lightness fizzed out of Tristan's mood. The fucker had followed him here? Was there no damn limit? He refused to turn around and look, so he asked, "Young Chinese guy? Be pretty hot if he wasn't an obvious psycho?"

Tristan should have known better, because now Shane was frowning at him, protective instincts clearly gearing up. "You having a problem with him?"

Tristan forced a laugh. "No, it's not a big deal. I've got it under control." Shane's squint showed that he wasn't fooled, so Tristan let go of the act and said, "Seriously, Shane, this is not one you want to get involved in. The guy is connected. *Very* connected. You trying to scare him off isn't going to work, and it would get both of us in way more trouble than we've got now."

"What kind of trouble do we have now, exactly?" Shane's voice was dangerously calm.

"It's just a nuisance. He wants me to work for him—or for his dad, or his uncle, or whatever. They're a pretty big family, and they're connected to other families. You know?"

"Triad?"

Tristan shrugged. He really tried to avoid any association with organized crime, and in Seattle it wasn't usually that difficult. So he didn't know all the details, not for sure. But what he believed? "Maybe not officially, but I think they've got relationships in that area, yeah."

"So how do you want to handle it?"

"I want to ignore it and hope it goes away," Tristan said. It was true, although probably not all that likely to work.

Shane didn't look even remotely satisfied by the plan. "You're *sure* he's connected?"

"I'm not sure about Triad, but his family? Shane, he's driving a brand-new Benz around. Seem like a typical low-level pimp to you?"

Clearly it didn't, but just as clearly Shane wasn't willing to follow Tristan's forget-it-and-hope plan. "How long's this been going on?"

Tristan sighed. Now Shane was going to be upset because he hadn't been notified earlier. "His guy talked to me last week. Really polite, just a business deal. Said he could hook me up with new clients, take care of things for me. I said I liked being an independent, he said I should rethink that, I said no. Same guy showed up the next day, that time with this guy along for the ride. A bit more pressure that time, and mentions of the family. And since then? Nothing big. I'm just seeing this guy around town, way more often than makes sense. He's not doing anything, just— watching. It's creepy, but not a big deal."

"I don't like it," Shane said, in a way that suggested he was planning to do something stupid.

"It's my deal, Shane. I'll handle it my way. If I need you, I'll let you know, but don't go charging into my business without me asking you to."

Shane looked ready to rebel. "Ignoring it isn't going to work."

Unfortunately, he was right. And, just as unfortunately, he was going to get himself hurt if he tried to take on the Triad single-handedly. So Tristan decided to play to his strengths. A sweet smile for Shane, then an even sweeter one as he jogged across the road to the Benz.

The driver didn't even look surprised to see him coming, which was a bit annoying. And the bastard didn't roll down his window, just left Tristan standing there in the street, waiting for him.

Tristan's already-fake smile was feeling completely frozen by the time the guy gave a tiny nod and then jerked his head toward the passenger side of the car.

That hadn't been Tristan's plan. He wanted to talk in public, not climb into the psycho's car. But he could hear Shane coming up behind him, ready to start yelling or smashing headlights or whatever other nonsense he could think of, and Tristan knew that would lead to disaster.

He hated his plan already, but he had to keep going with it. So he scampered around the back of the car, brushing past Shane in his full mother-bear protective mode, and found that the driver had leaned over and pushed the passenger door open. Tristan darted inside, yanked the door shut, and heard the lock click just as Shane's hand grabbed the outside handle. Oh, Shane didn't like this, and Shane was almost certainly right.

But Tristan's decision had been made.

The Benz glided out into traffic, away from angry Shane and disapproving Micah, and Tristan turned in the seat so he could get a better look at the driver. This was going to be interesting.

*****

Simon Yeung believed in being prepared. His uncle, who ran the family business and had raised him from birth, also believed in Simon being prepared. Simon wasn't one of Frank Yeung's natural children, so he needed to be useful in order to be accepted. Frank had never hidden that truth, and Simon had never doubted it.

So it made no sense for Simon to be driving down the street with the beautiful blond whore beside him, because taking the kid for a ride had *not* been part of the plan. Maybe later, if the whore continued to resist the family's business proposals, he'd be taken somewhere private and taught a few lessons about gratitude and respect. But Simon couldn't do that now, when there'd been hundreds of witnesses seeing the whore climbing into Simon's car, perfectly healthy. No, Simon's uncle would not be impressed with the way things were happening, here. The way Simon was *allowing* things to happen.

"So, how've you been?" the whore asked, his voice deliberately saccharine and light. "What have you been up to? Stalked anyone interesting lately?"

"Not that interesting, no," Simon replied. "Just another spoiled little duck who doesn't have the sense to take advantage of someone's generosity."

"Not really generosity if you have to *force* someone to take it."

"So you agree that I *could* force you, if I decided to?" Simon glanced over to get a look at the whore's expression. This was an important point, really. Was he being rebellious because he didn't know who he was dealing with, or was something else going on?

The whore just raised an eyebrow, then pointed out the windshield of the car. "You see that little girl up there on her bike? Looks about eight years old?" He paused to allow Simon to find the child, then said "*She* could probably force me into doing something, if we're just talking about playing rough. Seriously, I am not a tough guy, not at all."

"But you have tough-guy friends, and you think they can help you?" Simon asked, thinking of the punk who'd been chasing after the car.

"No," the whore said, just a little too quickly. "My friends aren't part of this."

"They will be if I decide they should be." So that was useful information. The whore was protective of his friends—a vulnerability.

"Jesus," the whore said. "Why is this such a big deal? I mean, I'm good at my job, sure, but it's not like I'm *that* good. If you're just looking to recruit a few new employees, I can ask around and see if anyone's interested. But as it is? You made an offer; I said no. Why can't we both just walk away?"

Simon needed to be smart about this, and there was nothing to be gained by getting into an argument. Still, if he could solve this whole issue right now, it would be one less headache for him in the days to come. So he drove with a little more purpose, but didn't bother answering the question.

"What, are you giving me the silent treatment, now?"

The whore waited for about half a block. "Seriously, we aren't even going to talk?"

Another half-block. "Well, this is totally pointless then, isn't it? Can you just drop me back at the park?"

They made it at least two more blocks before "Okay, it doesn't have to be back at the park. You can just let me out here—"

The car slowed for a light and the whore reached for the door handle. Simon reached over and caught his wrist. Warm skin, the bones close to the surface, but not as frail as the whore pretended to be. "Stay put," Simon said. "We're almost there."

"Almost where?"

"Where we're going."

The whore's body stayed tense for longer than Simon had thought it would, but his conditioning eventually kicked in and he relaxed. If something was going to be done to you, it was generally best to resist as little as possible. A good whore knew that.

They drove silently for another few blocks before pulling into the parking lot at the motel. It was owned by the family, and they kept a room around the back for private business.

The whore didn't seem impressed. "A motel? Seriously? Okay, but I charge a hundred bucks an hour, two hour minimum. For you, though? Two hundred bucks an hour."

"I know what you charge," Simon said. "That's how I know it's stupid of you to be turning down our offer, since you'd be making more with us *and* having more security."

He pulled into the spot in front of the room and looked over at the whore, who was looking back at him, a squint pulling his finely arched brows into—well, into brows that were arched just as finely, but at a different slant. "So, seriously, we're here to fuck? Is that what this is all about?"

"Come inside," Simon said. It was strangely pleasant to have the whore off-balance and confused. Simon was supposed to do his job because it was his job, not because he enjoyed it, but there was something about this situation tempting him to mix a little pleasure into his business. But, no. Uncle Frank wouldn't approve of that.

Still, he let himself fall behind the whore as they walked the few short steps to the motel room door and took a quick moment to admire the lean, lithe body in front of him. And when the whore stopped at the locked door and waited, Simon leaned over his shoulder to use the key card instead of edging around beside him. A good opportunity to be up close, to take an illicit sniff of the warm skin of the whore's neck…

But then the lock beeped and lit up green, the whore pushed the door open and went inside, and the moment was over.

Simon took a moment to collect himself before he stepped into the room and closed the door behind him. He was in charge of this meeting.

So he looked at the whore and didn't look away. He wanted to see the reaction. Then he pulled out his wallet, not even looking down as he pulled two bills from where the hundreds should be and took a half-step forward to drop the money onto the foot of the bed. The widening of the whore's eyes was satisfying.

"Take off your shirt," Simon said. His voice came out a little lower than he'd intended.

"One of the best parts of being an independent is that I can pick my own clients." The whore's hands didn't move to his shirt.

Simon just grinned at him. "One of the best parts of not being stupid is I don't talk business if I think someone might be wearing a wire. So if you want to talk this through, you'll need to get naked and watch me put your clothes and everything else you're carrying outside the door."

The whore frowned at him. "Who says I want to talk it through? I just want you to leave me the fuck alone!"

"And you plan to achieve that goal through persuasion and conversation, don't you? Isn't that why you got in my car?"

"I honestly have no idea why I got in your car."

"Maybe you just felt like wasting my time?" Simon let his gaze sharpen. He wasn't above taking advantage of the typical *gwai lo* attitudes—if racist whites thought Chinese faces lacked expression and could be cold? Well, he'd show them non-expressive and cold. But he didn't seem to be having much of an effect on the whore.

"Maybe. Maybe I feel like you're wasting *my* time, following me around like you have been."

Simon tamped down the flair of irritation. He was supposed to be calm and efficient; there was room for emotion in business, but only at the top levels. At Simon's level? He was a tool, and tools didn't get irritated. "Please, then." He gestured toward the door. "Don't let me keep you."

"And this is over? We're done, now?"

"The meeting? The meeting never really began, as I recall. So, it's almost a philosophical question at this point—can something that never existed be said to be over?"

"Not the meeting. The rest of it."

"I can't see why anything that happened this afternoon would have any impact on anything else that's happening in your life. After all, nothing really happened this afternoon, right? Are we back to the philosophy? Can something that never existed have an impact on something that does exist?"

"So, I get naked or you bore me to tears with cut-rate pseudo-zen bullshit?"

"What is the sound of one duck quacking, little duckling?"

"Enough with the 'duck' stuff. I know what it means, but are you even *from* China? Or Hong Kong or whatever?"

"If I were, your comments about my zen bullshit would be horribly culturally insensitive, wouldn't they?"

"I'm honestly supposed to be culturally sensitive to some Triad-connected pimp trying to strong-arm me into whoring for him instead of for myself?"

"If you can't be true to your principles when you're angry, are they truly your principles? Or are they just some cut-rate pseudo-hipster bullshit?"

The whore stared at Simon, and Simon stared back. Finally the whore said, "What the hell do you know about my principles?"

"You live like a peasant even though you make enough to live much better. You spend time with people who are going nowhere, even though you yourself could have a bright future, and are, in fact, planning for one. And you refuse a valuable business offer, one that would actually help you earn that bright future, because you think it's more important that you stay independent." He'd already said too much, but he didn't think the whore realized it. Which meant he could stop talking and go back to his plan. He didn't have to continue improvising. "So I know at least a little about your principles. The part where you'd think you were culturally sensitive was just an educated guess."

"My friends aren't going nowhere."

What a strange part of the speech to focus on. But Simon had gotten past his burst of loquacity. "Time will tell," was all he said.

The whore was beautiful when his face was relaxed, smiling at his friends. But he was something else altogether when his eyes blazed as they did there in the dingy motel room. Something that would be burned into Simon's memory for a very long time.

"I'm done with you," the whore said. "This is over. All of it. I'll stop working altogether before I work for you, and maybe you're right that the cops won't do much to help protect a whore from a pimp, but they'll do more to protect someone who *isn't* a whore anymore." He pulled the hem of his shirt up in a bravado display of his wireless chest. Listening devices were so small these days that the show meant nothing; the mike could have been hidden in countless places in his clothes, or on his body. But it was still a nice show. "I came to this meeting in good faith. But I guess it was pointless, because there's really nothing to talk about. There are no compromises to be reached. I won't work for you. Not ever." He stepped a little closer and practically whispered as he said, "I understand that it's not a word you hear too often, but you need to hear it now, and believe it." He waited for an appropriately dramatic moment, then said, "No."

He turned and started for the door. Simon said, "You know how to get in touch with me, don't you? When you decide you've changed your mind?"

"I'm not going to decide that."

"So you won't take my card with you? I really think it might be useful."

The whore was suspicious, now. He knew he was being set up, or maybe just bluffed, but he didn't know what to do about it and fell back on his obstinacy. "I don't need your card."

Simon nodded. "I'll tell you what. Tomorrow evening, say—eight o'clock? I'll send a car around for you. I think by then you'll realize that we really do have a few things to discuss. If you'd still like to try this without talking, that's your choice. But I think you'll get in the car."

"I think you're going to be really, really surprised," the whore said.

And Simon smiled as he said "Time will tell," again.

About the Author

Kate Sherwood started writing about the same time she got back on a horse after almost twenty years away from riding. She'd like to think she was too young for it to be a midlife crisis, but apparently she was ready for some changes!

Kate grew up near Toronto, Ontario (Canada) and went to school in Montreal, then Vancouver. But for the last decade or so she's been a country girl. Sure, she misses some of the conveniences of the city, but living close to nature makes up for those lacks. She's living in Ontario's "cottage country"–other people save up their time and come to spend their vacations in her neighborhood, but she gets to live there all year round!

Since her first book was published in 2010, she's kept herself busy with novels, novellas, and short stories in almost all the sub-genres of m/m romance. Contemporary, suspense, scifi or fantasy–the settings are just the backdrop for her characters to answer the important questions. How much can they share, and what do they need to keep? Can they bring themselves to trust someone, after being disappointed so many times? Are they brave enough to take a chance on love?

Kate's books balance drama with humor, angst with optimism. They feature strong, damaged men who fight themselves harder than they fight anyone else. And, wherever possible, there are animals: horses, dogs, cats ferrets, squirrels… sometimes it's easier to bond with a non-human, and most of Kate's men need all the help they can get.

After five years of writing, Kate is still learning, still stretching herself, and still enjoying what she does. She's looking forward to sharing a lot more stories in the future.

Find out more about Kate Sherwood and her books at her website: www.katesherwoodbooks.com

Follow Kate Sherwood on Facebook here.

www.ingramcontent.com/pod-product-compliance
Lightning Source LLC
Chambersburg PA
CBHW071119170626
46809CB00002B/427